TERRIFYING QUESTIONS, ELUSIVE ANSWERS

Was her husband John a pleasant, cheerful young engineer—or a dangerous manipulator in a bloody game of espionage?

Was charming, handsome Ian Haysrath a prospective lover—or was he a cunning enemy waiting for the moment her guard was down?

Were the servants in her new home acting as her protectors from a menace creeping ever closer in the desert night—or her captors in a prison of peril?

Fran was an innocent American in a world of international double-dealing—searching for a buried truth while the sands of time ran out. . . .

THE DRIFTING SANDS

Elsie Lee

A DELL BOOK

Published by
Dell Publishing Co., Inc.
1 Dag Hammarskjold Plaza
New York, New York 10017

ISBN: 0-440-11753-4

Printed in the United States of America
First Dell printing—August 1978

1

The plane came down in Lisbon and again in Cairo, and just as I felt I should burst if I had to wait another minute to see John, we landed in Qeman. Through the plane window I could see him loping back and forth behind the barriers like a caged lion—which he rather resembles, if lions ever had crewcuts and graduated from Princeton.

There's a particular charm about John. He's tall and tawny-colored and overpoweringly handsome—and utterly unaware of his effect on people. His face lit up like a child spying a lollipop as I tumbled down the landing steps into his arms, and I thought briefly that I should go away more often, just for the pleasure of coming back.

"You've had your hair cut," he said as soon as he'd kissed me.

"I thought it would be comfortable for a hot climate. Like it?"

"Very much," he approved. "What a girl you are, Fran! I'll bet you went through the import lists of Arabia and bought cases of whatever can't be bought here for love or money."

"Of course. And Mother sent a refrigerator."

"We've already got two—one for the kitchen and one for parties. Bet you won't find *that* in Toledo!" He grinned, turning me toward the airport inspection room.

I couldn't help laughing at his triumphant expression. Mother adores John, but she cannot conceal her amazement at my preferring to move from post to post with him, instead of staying in the comfort and stability of Ohio. "Mother says, sometimes she can't help wishing I hadn't married a nomad," I told him, straight-faced.

John choked slightly. "If she knew how much my degrees cost me, she'd be more respectful to mining engineers."

"Oh, she knows it was expensive," I returned serenely. "What she can't understand is why it doesn't look like more—if I make myself clear? She can explain a son-in-law in Panama or Venezuela, but Timor and Madagascar—the Ladies' Aid has never heard of them, and they waver between a suspicion that they were specially created to furnish jobs for the Kennetts, and a burning curiosity to know what we've done to be hidden away like remittance men."

His face was vaguely troubled as he pushed open the door to the inspection room. "Not much of a life for you, is it? Moving about so far from civilization . . ."

"Cheer up," I said lightly. "We're young, we're together—and we're not so out of the world as you think. Nita's somewhere in the Mediterranean this summer. Maybe we can get together before she goes home."

Anita Janus had been my college roommate, and to my unending joy, she and John had always thoroughly approved of each other. His face cleared now. "That would be great!"

An Arab in Western clothes moved forward, smiling. "Mr. Kennett? You follow, please?" Obediently, we worked our way through the passengers, who were milling around in the usual disorder—half of them obviously feeling certain all their luggage had been left behind in Cairo, and the other half resigned to outrageous Fortune.

A white-clad porter materialized through a side door, bearing the bare essentials I'd felt, in Toledo, I couldn't live without—and I already knew the excess-baggage costs would equal the cost of Paris original, thank you. In a split second we were on one side of the long counter, the bags spread before us and our guide whisked to the opposite side. "Your keys, Mrs. Kennett, if you please? Ah, thank you . . ."

They never was such VIP treatment—at least, I'd never had it before. But a glance at John showed he took it all for granted. He looked a bit taller than usual, though, and to my wifely eye this immediately indicated that he was carrying off A Situation.

I played up as best I could without a script, of course, plastering a Lady Vere de Vere expression on my face. I was leaning negligently against the counter, staring into space, when a nasal voice complained, "Pretty mean, honey! Why couldn't you get mine through with yours?"

Perforce I said to John (who was looking as though he *thought* there was a worm in this apple), "Darling, this is Ross Elvig. He's a photographer on an assignment for *Life*. Ross—my husband, John Kennett."

"Howd'ya do?" said John, extending a manly hand about on a lever with Ross's chest.

"Hi!" said Ross airily, reaching up with two languid fingers.

"Good trip?" John inquired.

"Fabulous!" Ross told him heartily. "Of course, it'd have been dull as ditchwater without Fran. Life of the party, she was."

"She always is," John agreed blandly. "One of her greatest qualities."

Well, I don't know where it would have ended, although it certainly looked like bared bodkins at half a pace tomorrow morning, but fortunately the inspector fumbled the final case containing my photographic materials, and Ross suddenly went natural and howled frantically, "Oh! My God, Kennett, *stop him!* He'll ruin the lenses . . ."

Startled, John swung about to the inspector, who went *café au lait* with apologies and explanations, while I examined the case with Ross breathing down my neck. "Jeeeesus!" he said finally, "How you got it all packed away in there!"

"I designed it, and John got it made for me in Singapore," I said proudly. "It's supposed to withstand everything from earthquakes to tidal waves."

He was still intent. "Listen, this is fabulous! My God, Fran, I plead with you—let me have it copied, hunh? It's too great!"

"Be my guest! I'm only a rank amateur, you know."

He straightened up thoughtfully. "Can you take pictures with this stuff?"

"Why else would I have it?" I inquired with a dignity that was wasted on Ross. I hadn't shared a seat with him for two days without learning that he was totally impervious to anything that got in the way of whatever he was pursuing.

"Yeah, sure," he said absently, running his hand over his stubby chin. "You do your own developing and printing, hunh?" I said nothing; certainly he could see by the pans and powder packets that I did. "Listen"—he grabbed my elbow urgently— "you'll be a pal and give me a hand? You know the lousy jobs in these foreign places? Half the time they ruin the negative so you have to reshoot everything, but this is one assignment that's all or nothing. . . ."

John turned about and looked astonished at the apparent intimacy. Hastily, I pulled away. "I— don't know when I'll get around to setting things up," I said evasively. To John I said, "Ready, darling?"

"Yes." He put a long arm about me and turned to the side door through which the porter was already hustling my luggage. Over his shoulder he said formally, "Good luck with the assignment, Mr. Elvig. Goodbye."

I could have told him no one gets rid of a news photographer that easily!

"Oh, you'll be seeing me again, Mr. Kennett," Ross said cheerfully, trotting after us. "Fran's going to let me use her development stuff. You know, us photographers always stick together, okay? So long, Fran, and thanks a million."

"But . . ." I began feebly, but John's strong arm kept me going. In silence, we went out and crawled into the car, with the bags already piled behind us. As we started forward, John remarked evenly, "Really, honey, you have an affinity for picking up bounders! Do I gather Mr. Elvig is making a home away from home at our place?"

"No; of course not," I said irritably. "I don't want him around any more than you do. I've already had two days of him. But he wants to borrow my darkroom for the films he's shooting for *Life*."

"Out of the question!"

"Yes, but the thing is, he's right about foreign processing. You know that was why I finally learned to do it for myself, John . . . and he *is* a top name in photography, and it *is* a *Life* assignment, after all."

"So let *Life* arrange to get his pictures developed."

"Aside from being a nuisance to have underfoot—and I'll agree he's exactly the sort to declare himself in on a pass—have you any other objection?"

"In a way," John said slowly, "yes—I have, Fran. I'd just . . . rather not have a total stranger around the house at the moment."

"Oh? Well then—'nuff said," I told him. Sliding across the front seat, I abandoned Ross Elvig in favor of the solidity of John's shoulder against my cheek. "Did you miss me?" I asked softly.

"Yes and no." (John's middle name is Honest.) "Everybody's been wonderful, and this is the nicest house we've ever had, honey. You'll be crazy about it! But this foreign colony is—different. I *think* you'll like it."

"But you don't sound too sure. What's wrong?"

Frowning, he concentrated on avoiding a couple of camels. "It's more than the usual nerves of a group of people away from home and hemmed in by protocol," he said after a moment. "I can't put my finger on it, Fran. Perhaps it's pure imagination. . . ."

But usually John wouldn't see a hidden situation if it were illustrated, and I felt puzzled during the rest of our drive. When we drew up before the house, I forgot everything else.

It was dazzling white stucco, with green awnings shimmering in the heat haze. I'd expected to be sitting in the middle of a desert, so it was a shock to find palm trees, a semblance of grass, and plenty of flowering bushes in the courtyard. There was a sort of wading pool, and the rooms were air-conditioned.

The servants looked unusually clean and intelligent. There were dozens of them, of course. In Eastern countries, you aren't supposed to change a light bulb for yourself—and the only person who can do it for you is a special boy in charge of changing light bulbs.

It is probably my undisciplined mind, but I suspect that foreign natives could teach even an American labor union a thing or two about loading payrolls.

The head of the servants was Ibrahim, a suave six-footer who spoke impeccable English and who sailed forward with white robes billowing about him like the sails on a weatherly ship. With a polite bow, he took me under his wing and conducted a tour of the house. John followed behind, like a hopeful puppy waiting for a kind word.

Upstairs and down we went. Here was the linen, here the household supplies; the switches for air conditioning and the mechanics of the laundry chute were demonstrated. This was Mr. Kennett's suite, and here were the morning room, bedroom, bath, and dressing room for Mrs. Kennett. I forbore telling Ibrahim that the Kennetts were far more accustomed to a *Baba Yaga* house on chicken-leg stilts and that we rather like sharing a bedroom—which was one reason we'd got married in the first place.

I knew that even when every blessed garment I owned had arrived by surface shipment, I'd never in the world have enough clothes to fill all the closets. I got out of it rather neatly, I thought, by saying that the largest closet would "do" for a darkroom. I could, I said nonchalantly, sacrifice it to My Art. This satisfied Ibrahim, but turning quickly, I caught a twinkle in John's eye and had a hell of a time keeping my face straight.

Eventually we got back to the main hall and a lineup of the staff—all dusky-skinned, white-clad, obsequious, and totally indistinguishable one from another. But it's only in America that you dare call all Pullman porters "George." In foreign parts you learn to tell who is which, and damned fast if you expect to get any service out of them.

So I went along the line and memorized names by my own unorthodox methods. Fatuoma had pierced ears and tiny gold rings; Selim was fat and had a gold tooth; the number-one boy was Fouad, with a small scar near his right ear. . . . John just stood in the background and looked tall, but apparently I passed with Ibrahim. When we'd finished, he said, "On behalf of the others and myself, Mrs. Kennett, I wish to welcome you to this house. It will be our pleasure to serve you and Mr. Kennett."

He made an even lower bow than originally and snapped his fingers gently, just once, and all the other servants practically fell on the tiled floor as they bowed. Then they filed out wordlessly, with Ibrahim bringing up the rear. It was evident he had the staff under his thumb, so all that was necessary was for me to get him under my thumb— although somehow I didn't think this would be too easy.

"How did we happen to get this dream of a house?" I asked John when we were alone. "I thought we were stuck in Tananarive for the next two years. Do you know Arabic or something?"

" 'Something,' " he told me seriously. "Technically, I'm on loan to the Sheik of Qeman as special consultant on salt deposits. This house belongs to the company."

"Oh." I thought I understood. The American Ambassador to Qeman was Mr. Baker, who'd been an executive of Madison Mines & Exploration. What with all the oil oozing out of Arabia, he was a more sensible choice than usual. John had worked for him in Texas before we were married and before John began to specialize in mining work for the company. The connection seemed easy. "Top-secret deals?" I asked.

"You know nothing," John said firmly. "I was in line for transfer, and it came through. That's all."

"All right," I said agreeably. "Just now I only want to know if you still love me."

His reply was immensely satisfactory, though not to be shared with outsiders. . . .

That was a night of enchantment. There was a delicious dinner, perfectly served, with subtle flavors tickling my Toledo palate. There was a sultry moon in a limitless carpet of stars as we drank coffee in the shadowy garden. The still desert air was pierced by weird sounds—a snatch of mournful native music, the whine of a dog sounding oddly

unlike dogs in Ohio. My imagination conjured up
jinns all about us.

While we were getting ready for bed, I said
idly, "I suppose Qeman isn't a good place for a
baby."

"God, no!" John said emphatically. "We're not
going through all that again, are we, Fran?"

We'd agreed to wait until we hit a good climate
or until I was twenty-eight, whichever came first.
But while I suspected Arabia wasn't a good climate, John seemed more vehement than necessary.

"Time's awasting," I said perversely. "We want
children, don't we?"

Turning, he gripped my shoulders, his hands
hard through the folds of my nightgown. "I won't
have you tied down, caught in a trap," he said
grimly. "Dragging small children from one outland-
ish spot to another . . . unhealthy, polyglot little kids . . . and not enough money for you to
get out if you weren't happy."

I stared at him incredulously. "You talk as
though I were going to leave you someday, John."

"You might want to," he returned. "Do you
think I could bear it if you wanted to and
couldn't?"

I thought that one over for a few days while I
unpacked and got into the routine of Qeman. Like
most hot climates, business was early in the morning and late in the afternoon, separated by a long
siesta. I like to keep an eye on the household, so

one morning I presented myself in the kitchen at 6 A.M. The staff was thrown into the wildest disorder, of course, until Ibrahim appeared.

"Good morning, Mrs. Kennett. You wished something?"

"Good morning, Ibrahim. I'm ready to go marketing."

Anyone who's lived abroad knows this is the sacrosanct privilege of the chief servant, and it's more than the kickbacks. In fact, it is the ultimate status symbol, and to interfere with it is to cause your most important servant to lose face.

Furthermore, unless you speak the language colloquially and are an accomplished bargainer, you won't save a penny and you'll waste three hours—because time is not the same in all parts of the world. There's lots more of it, apparently, the farther East you go. I've sometimes wondered whether this was not the initial observation that prompted Einstein's theory, although I never heard that he lived in the Orient. . . .

However, Ibrahim didn't bat an eyelash. "Of course, madam," he agreed. Gently, he snapped his fingers, and behind him the staff straightened itself out and quietly fell to work; he did not even glance at them. "It is usually Fouad who markets, but perhaps today—because of the language—I should come with you."

"If you wish, but Fouad is to market as usual." I turned to the door. "I'd like coffee, first."

It was Fouad who brought it, and I looked at him critically. Obviously, he was the lad who was getting the loot—and probably splitting with Ibrahim. That's standard, too.

He was small and unusually dark for an Arab; I suspected a touch of the African tarbrush. Even apart from the cheek scar, he was not prepossessing. Although I couldn't see any spots on his white robes, I had a distinct impression that they were slightly soiled about the edges, and his brown eyes slid away from mine disconcertingly.

Fouad spoke English after a fashion. He said now, "You ring when finish', I ready any time."

I took a full fifteen minutes. It was pleasant in the garden. An Eastern dawn doesn't have the dewy, sweet-smelling coolness of the Occident, but any dawn anywhere always has a sense of expectancy.

Finally, I rang for the servants, picked up a shade hat, and went out to the car. Selim was at the wheel; Ibrahim towered beside the open rear door. Thoughtlessly, I made my first slip. "Where's Fouad?"

"He will meet us at the market; there is no room for him in the car."

Automatically, I opened my mouth to say, "No *room?* Why, there's the whole back seat!" Just in time I caught Ibrahim's eye, and said instead, "If there is time, perhaps you'll show me the English bookshop."

Climbing into the back seat to ride in lonely state, I seethed inwardly. With a fifteen-minute head start, Fouad was now racing from shop to shop; the kickbacks must be superb if Ibrahim was so unwilling to lose them!

Then suddenly, wobbling along ahead of us on an ancient bicycle, was Fouad. We whirled past in a cloud of dust. Selim waved genially and shouted something that was unquestionably obscene, judging by Fouad's face. Ibrahim looked impassively into space, and I spent the rest of the drive in mental apologies. I still supposed he was getting a healthy share of the profits, but if his control of the staff was any indication, Ibrahim probably had all the tradesmen in his pocket too.

There was time for the bookshop and a glance at the native shops, and as always, I was so fascinated that I went farther and farther into the bazaar, until Ibrahim said, "Mrs. Kennett, Fouad will be waiting. . . ."

"I just want to see that rug shop across the way," I said, heading toward it eagerly, but Ibrahim swiftly stood in my path.

"If you please, madam—another day, perhaps."

I was about to protest, when I realized that I was out of bed at this ungodly hour only in order to make my presence felt. "Of course," I agreed docilely. Then, looking back to fix the rug shop in my mind, I was only too thankful. Ross Elvig was coming out of the place.

He hesitated in the shadowy doorway, looking this way and that with an odd wariness, and I turned hastily before he might identify me. At the corner I glanced back cautiously, but he was gone. Idly, I wondered about his assignment. What I'd

seen of the native quarter in Qeman seemed
scarcely worth a *Life* article, but of course, they'd
covered so much by now that they are scraping
the bottom of the barrel, at times.

Fouad was just dismounting at the meat shop.
Within, the store was crowded with the principal
servants of the foreign colony. My appearance,
naturally, cast a funereal pall over the place.
Fouad strode forward with a swagger indicating
the deepest humiliation, and a campstool was produced.

I sat down with dignity, and the meat man was
brought forward to be presented. Through Ibrahim, I informed him graciously that, being new to
Qeman, I had wished to know personally all our
suppliers, that Fouad would, of course, continue
to handle our purchases, and that we placed entire
confidence in his ability.

That was that. Fouad put on a fine show and
got everything at very good prices—*that* day.
From shop to shop we went, like a royal progress,
but eventually we were done, and Fouad was dispatched to return the campstool to the meat market. Ibrahim held open the car door for me, and
simultaneously I heard a familiar nasal twang.
"Fran, how're you, sweetie! Long time no see."

It was Ross. "How are you?" I returned.
"Thought you'd be communing with camels by
now."

"Nah, not yet. This is a tricky deal," he said, his
face suddenly intent. "Listen, whereya going?"

"Just home."

"Great! I'll ride along. I could use a cup of coffee—okay?" Before I could think of an excuse, he'd pushed me into the car, piled in after me, and slammed the door in Ibrahim's face.

The Arab hesitated, his eyes on me. Quickly I said, "Home, Selim," and Ibrahim slowly got into the front seat, wrapping his robes about him neatly.

As the car started forward, "How do you like Qeman?" we chorused, and laughed irrepressibly.

"Opening gambit number one," he said. "You first—how do *you* like it?"

"I love it," I said sincerely. "We're living in a plush-bottomed oasis; wait'll you see. What about you?"

"Personally, I'm just a Brooklyn boy at heart. Give me little old New York." He shrugged. "How's the darkroom?"

"I . . . haven't set it up yet."

"What's to set up?" he asked in surprise. "Listen, give me the stuff and show me where, and I'll fix it for you."

"Well, as a matter of fact, I'm not sure . . . that is," I floundered, "I don't think you'd better count on using it."

He eyed me sharply. "Boss man objects?"

"I've been marketing," I said clearly. "You know it's wonderful how many Arabs speak English, and better than a lot of people back home."

"I get you," he muttered, and relaxed slightly.

"Ibrahim took me to the English bookstore, and we went into the bazaar," I went on, at random.

"By the way, does that rug shop have anything good?"

There was a fractional pause. "Rug shop?"

"Yes—I saw you coming out of it this morning."

"Not me, sweetie! I haven't been near the bazaar," he said positively. "Have you had a camel ride yet?"

We drew up before the house at that moment, and despite John's mandate, I swept Ross out to the garden and sent for coffee. "Now, what *is* all this?" I demanded. "You know very well I did see you this morning."

"Sure," he returned easily. "I was making arrangements for a desert caravan."

"What's so classified about that?"

"Ask me no questions and I'll tell you no lies," he said. "Maybe I want to go where they don't care for strangers."

"I see."

"Now you tell me why I can't use your darkroom," he countered. "You'll never get me to believe your husband is jealous of me!"

"No; of course not," I said carefully, "but you know foreign countries. We're newcomers; everyone loves to gossip; John doesn't want me to get off on the wrong foot, Ross."

"Ummmm." He drained his cup and let it dangle from one finger, frowning in concentration. Then he sat back and extended the cup. "May I have another?" As I refilled, he said, "By the way, it's stupid of me, but what's your husband's position—attaché?"

"Oh, he's not diplomatic; he's a mining engineer. Washington lent him to the Sheik as a consultant—something about salt deposits, I think."

"Madison Mines?"

"Yes," I admitted unwillingly.

"Interesting," he murmured. "I suppose he and Baker are old friends. No, don't tell me. I can add two and two as well as the next guy."

"There's nothing to add, really. We'd been in Madagascar for two years, John was in line for transfer, and this was it." Deliberately I carried the war into the enemy camp. "Tell about your assignment—I gather it's in the desert? When do you leave, and how long will it take?"

"I'm doing a layout on a nomadic Bedouin tribe, leave tomorrow, don't know how long it'll take," he said absently—but the words were as pat as mine. I wondered what Ross Elvig was *really* going after, but before I could think of another leading question, he'd set down his empty cup and stood up. "Thanks for the coffee." He smiled suddenly. "You're a good kid, Fran."

Brash and unshaven as he was, his smile was somehow sweet. Impulsively I said, "If you dare to trust me, perhaps I could process your films. . . ."

"Maybe." Pulling out a cigarette, he lit it, considering. "Listen," he said softly. "Tell your husband he's got nothing to worry about with me. I won't get in his way—and maybe, when I get back, I'll have something to interest him. About those salt deposits." He grinned at me ironically. "So long, sweetie—I can find my way out."

Then he was gone, brushing past Fouad, who was coming out to remove the coffee cups.

2

There was an enormous pile of visiting cards by the end of my first week in Qeman. It's always best to return duty calls at once—people can be awfully touchy when there isn't much else to occupy their minds. So I crawled into my best clothes every afternoon. Between the heat and the menace of native traffic, principally camels, it was a tiresome chore.

Fortunately, almost everyone was "not at home." Sir Percival Morton, dean of the diplomatic colony, was a widower, and Mr. Baker, whom John was mysteriously assisting, was in Basra. I had grown so used to dropping cards, crossing off a name, and proceeding to the next house, that it was a shock to be smilingly ushered into the French Consulate.

The room to which I was shown was cluttered with cheap Benares brass, Chinese ashtrays, some moth-eaten stuffed animals, a miscellany of palm fans, peacock feathers, and two magnificently carved aboriginal heads in polished mahogany. The decor bore witness to a long and varied service in diplomacy, but it was enough to give anyone the whimwhams in the torrid climate of Qeman.

I was examining the heads, when the door opened. "Madame Kennett?" a voice purred behind me. "I am madame Drouet. 'Ow do you do?"

"How do you do?" I said politely, shaking her plump, beringed little hand. I thought I should have known instantly anywhere that she was French. From her neat black chignon and sparkling, malicious black eyes, to her black dress and patent-leather pumps into which her figure and feet had been stuffed to the imminent danger of bursting every seam, madame Drouet shrieked *jolie dame de Paris*. "It is so kind of you to receive me," I said.

She chuckled wickedly and turned to tug at a bell-pull. "Oh, I know very well I should be 'not at home' and allow you to finish your list," she admitted slyly, "but then you 'ave only three more names. Oh, yes, I know," she went on, at my look of surprise. "The houseboy tell me. It is the grapevine, you know. 'We 'ave 'ad madame Kennett. 'Ave *you* 'ad madame Kennett?' And so everyone know, and I think you should rest and have a cool drink."

In half a minute I was seated opposite madame Drouet and completely under her spell.

· "Protocol!" she remarked darkly. "*Je m'enfiche de ça!* It is—how you say in America?—for the birds!" And she looked so pleased with herself that I swallowed my vermouth cassis the wrong way and nearly choked to death.

Despite her charm, though, it didn't take me ten minutes to realize that my hostess was a very skillful wormer-out of secrets. "And so your 'usband has come to Qeman for the oil," she said placidly.

But I hadn't chosen John instead of a dramatic career for nothing. "Oh, I don't think so," I returned, equally placid. "He was due for a transfer, and we'd hoped it might be Switzerland. We'd have liked Europe for a change."

Her black eyes sparkled for a second, then dropped below heavy, waxen eyelids. "*Alors,* how do you like Qeman?"

"Very much, so far."

"Ah, you are young—you do not mind the routine as yet." She nodding approvingly. "Everything is strange and interesting, and while you learn, you can overlook the people, *n'est-ce pas?*"

"If all the 'people' are like you, I shall have no difficulties," I said, smiling. "I look forward to meeting monsieur Drouet."

"You are interested in philately, madame Kennett?" she inquired with sudden animation.

Bewildered, I said, "No; I'm afraid I only use stamps when I write letters—and that isn't any more often than I can help."

"Too bad," she sighed regretfully. "Philately—it is Henri's passion, you understand? Otherwise, he rarely emerges." She took a sip of her own drink and looked at me thoughtfully. "He is a sweet young man, your John," she said. "Everyone has liked him at once. It was time you came."

"This is the first time we've been separated for more than a few days since we were married," I admitted.

"So?" Her dark eyebrows flew upward. "It is not good to leave a husband for long in these foreign places. It is . . . difficult . . . for a man to be alone. And have you met Mrs. 'Aysrath?"

Somehow I didn't think she had changed the subject. "No," I said guardedly. "She hasn't called as yet."

Sheila Haysrath came the next afternoon. "You don't *have* to see me, you know," she said in a bored, brittle voice. "I have to do protocol calls for the English Embassy because Sir Percival's sister has gone home for the summer."

She sat down languidly in the lounge chair—one of those thin, angular, blond women who fold up like a pocketknife when approaching a seat—and I rang for iced drinks.

"This is much nicer than the diplomatic houses," she remarked. "We're very glad John has it. We're all so fond of your husband, Mrs. Kennett. Even Ian likes him."

"Ian?"

"My husband. He almost never likes anybody," she said casually, "or anything but a whiskey bottle."

I was completely at a loss for words, but fortunately Ibrahim brought in the drinks at that moment.

"Don't ever let anyone tell you of the glories of the diplomatic corps, Mrs. Kennett," she went on, ignoring Ibrahim as though he were a floorboard. "I had dreams of glamorous palaces and high society once, and what did I get? I've been dragged around more second-rate principalities than I ever knew existed even in an atlas!"

"We haven't hit anything very glamorous yet, ourselves," I said temperately, "but there are always transfers."

She took a long pull at her Tom Collins. "Transfers!" Her staccato voice was more bored than ever. "Don't tell me! Take the children out of school, pack up everything we own—which isn't much, God knows—and wind up someplace worse than before."

"How many children do you have?" I asked, beginning to see daylight.

"Two—poor little beasts."

"Can't you send them home to England, to stay with your parents or go to school?"

She shook her head. "Parents all dead, and we can't afford school fees." She laughed shortly. "It costs a lot to keep an Englishman in liquor, you know."

"I'm . . . sorry," I murmured inanely.

"Don't be shocked," she returned more calmly. "It's no secret that Ian is drinking himself to death, and I'd leave him if I could. I wouldn't

have mentioned it, but John knows. He's seen . . .
things. . . ."

She put down her glass and rose to go, her thin
lips set in lines of discontent and self-pity. Under
the hard brilliance of her green eyes appraising
me, I felt chilled, unwelcome. "You're one of the
lucky ones," she said. "I'd give anything to have a
man like your John."

I looked her right in the eye. "*I* think he's nice
too."

She shrugged slightly. "He's a good friend. I've
cried all over him a couple of times, but he's wonderful about it."

When she had gone, I went across the hall and
burst into John's study; I knew he was home by
that time. "Are you refusing to let me have babies
because of Sheila Haysrath?" I demanded with no
preamble whatever.

He looked bewildered. "Well, she's a good ex-
ample of what can happen."

"I never heard anything so ridiculous!" I told
him. "*You* aren't drinking yourself to death, are
you, or beating me up on Saturday nights, or
whatever it is he does to her!" I stormed out and
slammed the door behind me.

Our first big invitation was that night, and I was
lying on the bed with lotion pads over my eyes,
while Fatuoma fussed around quietly. I'd never
had a personal maid before, and Fatuoma spoke
so little English that I couldn't really communicate with her, so I'd no idea where she had

learned her trade. From the way she took charge of me and my clothes, there was no doubt in my mind that she knew more about Qeman society than I did.

She had first set me in a chair, draped me with a sheet, and given me a facial massage. She had then authoritatively indicated that I should lie upon the bed, slapped the wet pads on my eyes, and quietly settled down to a fresh manicure.

So I was in semi-Nirvana when John came in and said, "I don't think you're quite fair to Sheila."

"What has that got to do with my having a baby?" I asked in surprise. "I'll agree she seems to have drawn a prize lemon for a husband—although it's a bit non-U for her to tell me all about it the first time we meet. But I can't see why her experience affects my life."

"Haysrath is a complete heel," John said fiercely. "I don't know, we none of us know, how she stands him. I'd better warn you, Fran—he'll probably even try to make passes at you."

"Well, thank *you*, Lord Chesterfield," I said lightly. "How many drinks will he need before he can stand me?" Throwing off the eye pads, I sat up and Fatuoma rushed forward with a robe, but John was looking out the window.

"You know what I mean," he said. "I'd like to suggest that you and Sheila should be friends. She needs friends badly. But I don't think you're the type to get along together. Sometimes you can be so—so—*uncompromising*, Fran."

That was when I knew for certain that madame Drouet had not changed the subject the previous afternoon.

I pulled the robe about me and said, "Hadn't you better dress? Heaven forbid we should be late on my first appearance."

"My God, yes," he said, and dashed for the shower. I was fastening my earrings when he returned, with a black tie draped over his fingers and an expression of infinite trust on his face. While I twitched the tie into place, he suddenly said, "What happened to Ross Elvig?"

"Probably in the desert, by now. I'm sorry, John; he nabbed me the day I went marketing and declared himself in for coffee, but he was leaving the next day."

"What's this assignment?"

"A layout on one of the desert tribes," I said slowly, remembering. "And he told me to tell you not to worry—he wouldn't get in your way, and maybe he'd have something to interest you when he got back."

John frowned. "What on earth . . . ?"

"I'm sorry I forgot to tell you. Is it important?"

"I doubt it—but I'd really rather you didn't get involved. There were some unsavory stories— native girls, and so on."

"I'm not surprised," I said uncomfortably, "but I offered to process his films for him, John."

"Tell Ibrahim to say you're not at home," John told me. "Come on; we'll be late."

The party that evening followed a pattern, I

gathered, of all previous parties and all that were to come. Cocktails, dinner, an hour of entertainment (tonight it was native music); then the ranking diplomat left and the older people swiftly followed, leaving the youngsters to dance to phonograph records and—in the case of Ian Haysrath—to get drunk.

Tonight was different only because I could fit names to faces, and naturally I had a burning curiosity about one or two people.

As pro tem hostess for the British Embassy, Sheila was definitely not exerting herself. She swam up to us as we entered, neatly cut John away to the far end of the room, and abandoned me to Sir Percival, who was the typical British ambassador and slightly hard of hearing to boot.

In rapid succession, I was making mental notes of the Italians (signor Francia—gold wedding ring and sideburns), the Greeks (madame Iandouros—Cinderella-sized feet and blue eyes), and the Russian Tomyienkovs, whose figures attested the difficulties of diet in the USSR. Gregor Semirov, their attaché, was unexpectedly young and slender.

After that, names and faces washed over me until madame Drouet surged forward. She was stuffed into a sausage casing of Schiaparelli pink, with masses of diamonds sparkling only one degree less than her black eyes.

"*Ma chére*," she said impressively, "for you, because I have told 'im about you, Henri has emerged!" The wave of her plump little hand produced the French Ambassador like a rabbit from a hat. "*Mon chou, je vous presente à madame Kennett.*"

Monsieur Drouet murmured, "*Enchanté, madame,*" but of course it was *I* who was enchanted. When I'd reported my visit, John had been scant help. He'd said only that Drouet was known to be in ill health and rarely attended any but essential diplomatic affairs. It was popularly accepted that madame actually ran the Embassy and that they were just marking time until his retirement next year.

There was no denying that monsieur Drouet closely resembled a bunch of second-day supermarket scallions—slightly wilted at the top and faintly yellow beneath—but as he bowed over my hand, I caught a rapier glance from his dark eyes, and I thought I wouldn't advise anyone to underestimate this man, ill health or not!

The other person of most interest was Ian Haysrath, and in the end he introduced himself. I was talking to Gregor Semirov and thinking privately that it was a pity he was a Communist, because just a touch of capitalist levity would have made him irresistible. Dinner had been announced, and a British voice said at my ear, "Mrs. Kennett? Ian Haysrath here. May I take you in to dinner?"

Startled, I swung about—to face the handsomest man I've ever seen anywhere! He was tall and perfectly proportioned, with dark, wavy hair and deepset eyes of incredible sapphire blue framed in a fantastic thicket of black eyelashes. Somehow

I'd assumed Ian Haysrath would be physically unattractive, to match his reputation.

I suppose the shock showed clearly on my face, for he smiled sardonically and said, "You *will* forgive my belated appearance? Yes, I feel sure that you will, that you *understand* all the myriad duties of an attaché."

I didn't much like the glint in his eye. "Why, of course I understand the myriad duties of an attaché," I said sweetly, "and I do hope you've cooked us a good dinner tonight, Mr. Haysrath?"

He stared at me appraisingly. "I might have known John'd have a wife like you," he said after a moment. "I imagine you always avoid the obvious with ease."

"Isn't John the proof of that? Shall we join the throng?"

When the dancing began, the men did their duty by me, but I wasn't too engrossed to notice that John had almost every dance with Sheila. She didn't seem to be a very good dancer, but since every stumble brought her closer to John, perhaps she had a reason.

Toward the end of the evening my partner went to get me a glass of water, and Ian Haysrath came up to me unsteadily. "Goin' to be quite a pleasant addition to our fold, Mrs. Kennett," he said indistinctly. "Keep John occupied, will you?"

"I hope so."

"Got to keep him out of Sheila's clutches," he confided with drunken wisdom. "M'wife's a hussy, Mrs. Kennett. Don't want ol' John to be another of her tomcats, eh?"

"I'm sure you needn't worry, Mr. Haysrath," I said politely, and made for the powder room. There's never any point to blowing your top with a drunk. When I returned, he was weaving among the dancers.

"We're goin'," he said abruptly to Sheila.

"You go," she said sulkily. "John will bring me home."

Ian grasped her shoulder and pulled her away from John. "Leave him alone," he said loudly, and called her something unprintable.

John grew white and clenched his fists, until I found my voice and said "John!" compellingly. Then he drew back and looked about blindly until I walked over and took his arm.

I wondered how much longer the mere sound of my voice would deter him. . . .

In the next few weeks John saw a lot of Sheila. It was all quite open and friendly. I put my pride in my pocket and tried to make friends with her myself, but it was obvious that she preferred male companions. She seemed to split her time between John and Gregor Semirov, and since Gregor wasn't married, I could only hope he had the inside track.

Ian was in and out of Qeman, on some unspecified "Embassy" business, which usually coincided with formal parties that argued that Sir Percival was more intelligent than he looked. But when-

ever Ian turned up at an informal evening, he in-
variably got drunk, and it was evident he and
Sheila led a cat-and-dog existence. John grew irritable and snapped at me over trivial matters in a
very upsetting fashion. To top it all, I was convinced that someone was systematically searching
my room.

It seemed absurd; I had no valuable jewelry,
and nothing was ever taken. I'd grown used to the
curiosity of native servants in other countries. I
told myself it was some downstairs maid, wanting
to see the colors in my closet. But if so, why
should it recur? And why should it include the
biggest closet, which I finally set up as a darkroom?

It might be Fatuoma, giving a conducted tour
of my wardrobe to impress her friends, but I
quickly realized she, too, had noticed the minute
displacements—the hairbrush mysteriously in the
wrong drawer, the ill-folded evening scarf. . . .
When Fatuoma noticed, she was puzzled but apparently satisfied that I had made the changes.
With pursed lips, she refolded the scarf, then shook
her finger at me sternly, and ended with a giggle
for her own audacity.

Against my will, I felt the search was un-
friendly. Yet why should anyone dislike me so
quickly after my arrival in Qeman? I was first re-
sentful, then frightened, by the sense of surveillance, but perhaps it was only my own jumpy
nerves, affected by the general tension. I said
nothing to John about it; he had enough on his

mind as it was—because the word had leaked out
about the oil negotiations.

Mr. Baker had returned from Basra. He and
John had worked late and—they thought—secretly;
yet next day everyone in Qeman knew all the details.

"And so your husband does not tell you all 'is
business?" madame Drouet purred that afternoon.
"You do not know of this oil contract when I tell
you that first day."

I flushed involuntarily, and she laughed. "I
make a little joke," she said, patting my hand gently. "It is *good* that a man's wife can be silent.
And so, we 'ave a spy among us!"

"Isn't it more likely a curious servant? Natives
gain face when they spread news about their em-
ployers."

"The native do not gain face if he lose his job,"
she pointed out. "And if too much is known about
this contract, it may—how you say?—queer the
pitch." As always, she looked innocently pleased
with her grasp of American slang, while I inwardly choked. Then her face went serious.
"Someone take trouble to find out what is going
on, and has a motive that it shall be known. That
is only a spy," she said shrewdly. "*Enfin,* I wonder
who it can be. . . ."

I wondered about it myself. At dinner I said to
John, "What is this contract, and who'd want to
prevent it?"

"Anyone," he sighed. "The Russians, of course,
and the nationalist Arab groups—they're always

the most likely. But any foreign country would be
interested to know what's going on."

"Madame Drouet?"

He nodded. "Anyone, Fran. Of course, it's possible some wildcat American outfit might think
that if they stirred up enough unrest over our
terms, they could sneak in with a better offer," he
said wearily. "Even today, with all the royalties
and conditions and restrictions, an oil contract
ain't hay, honey."

"But how do you know there's any oil there?"

"We don't," he said. "This is just the usual exploration contract—so much survey in two years,
so much in four years, followed by test wells. But
whoever gets the exploration contract, *if* he finds
oil, gets the exploitation contract too. A little guy
can't afford much exploration, but if he hits before the money runs out . . . well, it's worth the
gamble."

"I see," I said, and of course I did. Any mining
engineer's wife knows that the Near East is practically floating on oil—the stuff comes right out of
the ground and collects in *puddles*—so it was a
safe bet there was plenty more beneath Qeman.
All that was necessary was to sink the pipe in the
right spot.

"What's become of Elvig?" John asked suddenly.

"I don't know."

"If he turns up," he said slowly, "get anything
you can out of him, Fran. He's an American, after

all, and at this point . . . well, I'm not too proud to look for any help I can get."

I began to understand what John had said the day I arrived about the atmosphere in Qeman. We'd had scandals and social feuds in Puerto Rico and Mozambique, but the tension in Qeman increased daily. Whoever the spy was, he didn't catch every move, but the suspense of wondering which detail he'd get was awful.

The heat was thick and dry, where previously we'd had only damp heat. John and I used to make up lurid schemes when we couldn't sleep, for getting transferred to a nice cool spot like Norway. Most of them involved my appearing in sheer black lace and fascinating some important person, and they never came to anything because I am not that sort of girl.

I am the typical American type—tallish, thinnish, with the long legs GI's are supposed to dream about in foxholes. Since my legs are seen only in sport clothes, they contribute little to my glamor. The least touch too much makeup, and John tells me severely that I look like a totem pole; and heavy, seductive perfume makes my head ache. I have straight hair-colored hair and nondescript hazel eyes.

Definitely, I'm not fascinating; but since I've never cared to entice anyone but John, it doesn't really matter.

Ian Haysrath professed to disagree with this, and he developed an irritating habit of dropping in at teatime whenever he was in Qeman. Now that I could look at him more closely, I saw the faint marks of dissipation. There was a daredevil, rakehellish look about him that confused me. He was so inordinately handsome, so almost beautiful, that it was hard not to sit and simply feast the eyes. Yet I could not make up my mind whether the buccaneer's dash was innate or merely assumed as a means of convincing the world such a pretty man was still a *man*.

Certainly, he was an accomplished flirt. He always insisted on shaking hands and held my fingers for just a fraction too long. Aside from the intended significance, I detested shaking hands with him. His skin was dry but chill, and it seemed stretched too tightly, so that one felt one was shaking hands with a manicured parrot.

He seemed to assume we should console each other while John and Sheila were occupied elsewhere. "Two wrongs don't make a right," I told him.

"What's wrong in my callin' on you?" he asked innocently. "You're a very fascinatin' little woman, Fran."

"Nonsense!" I said shortly. "I'm a lot of things, Ian, but fascinating isn't one of them. And I'm not interested in a phoney, see-if-I-care flirtation, either."

"No, you wouldn't be," he agreed after a minute. "I'd forgotten there are women like you, Fran."

But he did not stop calling at teatime, which only added to the strain, since our house was be-

tween the airport and his home. The planes from
Cairo, Teheran, Damascus, and so on, all arrived
in a clutch about 4 P.M. each day, and Ian's appearance subtly implied tactfully killing time to
avoid arriving home at an awkward moment. . . .

He'd been away rather longer than usual when
he turned up about 5 P.M., just as I was about to
dress for the Italian Embassy dinner. To my astonishment, he was sporting a neat, dark mustache.
"Weren't you devilish enough?" I inquired, and
he laughed wickedly.

"I've been out of touch with a razor," he said. "I
finally got a shave, but I told them to leave the
mustache. I'd a fancy to see Sheila's face."

Well, there were a lot of flip answers to that
one, but he seemed in such a good mood that I
smiled and said, "You're simply gilding the lily,
you know!"

He sank into the patio chair with a sigh of con-
tentment and accepted the ginger ale I pointedly
handed him. "It's good to be back—even to a hell-
hole like this," he observed.

"It's not really so bad," I remarked. "You should
have seen Tananarive!"

"Life turns out differently from what one ex-
pects, doesn't it, Fran?" he said thoughtfully. "If I
hadn't gone to cram with a country vicar, I'd
never have met Sheila. . . . And if I hadn't met
Sheila, I'd never have thought of the diplomatic
service. But she pointed out that I could use Arabic and Hindustani in more ways than imports
and exports for my uncle."

In view of Sheila's sneers about palaces and glamor, I was surprised at his words. I'd definitely gathered that Ian had swept an innocent country girl off her feet by tales of glory ahead. And whatever Sheila had learned in the vicarage, it hadn't been housekeeping. Arab servants were heaven after the woolly-headed natives in Timor and Madagascar, but they still needed supervision.

With just as many servants as the rest of us, Sheila's house never looked quite clean; her food was sparse and grudgingly served; her children were always a little too soiled and sticky. In my nastier moments, I thought that such a dismal home might well drive any man to drink—but perhaps Sheila lacked the incentive to run a cheerful place because Ian so evidently didn't appreciate it.

"I'm going to throw you out as soon as you finish the drink," I told Ian now. "Italian Embassy tonight."

"Oh, *hell!*" he said wearily.

"Signora Francia's sister is giving us a recital of Tuscan folk song," I murmured naughtily.

"After thirty miles on camel back? Oh, my God!"

"I thought you came in by plane?"

He drained the glass, set it down with a thump, and stood up, stretching his shoulders, with a wince. "So I did," he returned casually, "but I had to use a camel for a taxi. Oh, well, thanks for the drink. See you later, Fran."

After he'd gone, I started once more for my

bedroom. Ibrahim was adjusting blinds and inspecting the living room with an expression that boded no good for Fouad, although I couldn't imagine what was substandard. To me, the place looked ready for *House Beautiful*.

"Good evening, Ibrahim," I said, and headed for the stairs, but to my surprise he followed.

"Mrs. Kennett," he said in an undertone, "the American has returned to Qeman."

"The American?" He nodded, his eyes fixed on the tile floor. "You mean Mr. Elvig? Did he come here?"

He shook his head. "I saw him in the native quarter this afternoon."

"Oh? If Mr. Elvig should call, Ibrahim, *both* Mr. Kennett and I will always be at home to him," I said deliberately, and was rewarded by a swift upward glance. I wondered how on earth Ibrahim had sensed John's initial dislike of Ross, but he said only, "Very good, madam," and bowed politely while I continued up the stairs.

Fatuoma had laid out my newest and most expensive evening dress—a clinging job of white silk jersey, cut a bit soon over the rear end and with a definite forward thrust of the chassis. I'd mentally dedicated this to the top-top affair, but I'd already learned that Fatuoma's judgment was infallible. Somehow she always knew what sort of evening lay ahead. After the evening when she'd forced me into my dowdiest dinner dress with long sleeves—and Sir Percival's "old school friend" had turned out to be the Anglican Bishop of Lambeth—I had never questioned her.

I was sitting at the dressing table, using hair lacquer on stray wisps, when John came in with a white tie and his usual expression of infinite trust.

"Ross Elvig is back," I told him.

"Oh?"

"Ibrahim saw him in the native quarter."

"Hmmmm."

"I told Ibrahim if Ross called, we were both at home at any time."

"Ah?"

"Oh, *you!*" I said crossly, and jerked at the tie. John choked slightly and grinned.

"Well, you always wanted to be an adventuress, didn't you?" He eyed me critically. "That's certainly the dress for it."

"If I weren't afraid of ruining Fatuoma's paint job, I'd kiss you," I said.

"Tell her to do it over again." He put his arms around me—and wouldn't you know, Fatuoma materialized from nowhere, to stand just behind my shoulder.

"Caaaar!" she said warningly, as we stared at her, she added, "No spoil!" Then she shook her finger sternly and broke apart in giggles.

"Good God, is she always like this?" John asked.

"Yes," I told him; "she doesn't care what I do after I get there, but I should arrive looking a credit."

For a moment he looked mutinous. Then he sighed resignedly and turned me to the door. "You lead a tough life, honey. She may not care what happens after you make the entrance—but in that dress, I can tell you, I *do*."

"Don't be absurd." I started down stairs, and behind me John gave a long American wolf whistle.

Ibrahim, standing ready to open the door, looked up involuntarily. I could feel myself flush, but I continued with what dignity remained—only to be undone when John folded my wrap about me and said jovially, "She's a knockout tonight, isn't she, Ibrahim?"

The Arab looked at him impassively, swung open the door, and bowed. "The staff is *always* proud of Mrs. Kennett's appearance, sir."

"That's one in the eye for you, my lad," I told John. "Thank you, Ibrahim." But I had a distinct impression of the beginnings of a twinkle in Ibrahim's eyes . . .

I saw immediately that Fatuoma had been right. Madame Iandouros was plastered with an indecent display of sapphires, and not much else—while madame Drouet wore a subtle sea-green brocade without a jewel in sight. Even madame Tomyienkov had a new dress of bronze rayon taffeta, above which her face was a desert sunset of inexpert *maquillage*.

The upper male echelon was white tie with decorations—but I'd have known it was gala anyway, because monsieur Drouet had "emerged." He bowed conventionally over my hand and said,

"It is good to see you again, Mrs. Kennett. Unfortunately, my health is not equal to society, but my wife tells me you enjoy Qeman. She takes great pleasure in your friendship."

"And I in hers," I returned warmly—but I thought it odd that it had never occurred to me to wonder why the French Ambassador spoke flawless Oxford English. It was only one of the shocks of that evening, and perhaps I should simply list them, for despite their confusing effect on my mind, each played its own part in what was to come.

There was, first, Ross Elvig, in traveler's dinner kit of dark suit, white shirt, and black tie; but for once he was unrumpled and shaved. He'd even added a dark red cummerbund, and when he turned up at my elbow during cocktails, I scarcely recognized him.

"What a difference Dial Soap makes!" He grinned.

"Ross! It's good to see you!" Oddly enough, it was true. He put an arm about my shoulders, hugged me briefly, and gave me a casual smack on the cheek—and it was all very American and normal. "I heard you were back. . . ."

"Not *me*, honey," he said, astonished. "I only rolled in half an hour ago. I'm staying here, did you know?" I shook my head wordlessly. "Sometimes I can be respectable, sweetie," he said lightly, but his eyes held a definite warning.

After that, the shocks came in rapid succession. Signora Francia's sister turned out to be Mon-

talva, the newest international opera sensation;
Gregor Semirov was my dinner partner, and he did
not fade away to Sheila as usual, once duty was
done . . . and Ian Haysrath did not get drunk!

As a party, it was a triumph. Oh, there were
some Tuscan folk songs among the encores, but
otherwise the entertainment was so superb that
we could not let Montalva go. It was as though
she were simply singing for friends, in the drawing room after a family dinner, and it ended with
everyone forgetting dignity and calling out personal requests.

She sang them all (her accompanist was fabulous), from Sir Percival's diffident suggestion of
"Hark, Hark, the Lark" to madame Drouet's demand for "Au Clair de la Lune." Only the Russians sat silent.

"Isn't there *something* you'd like her to sing?" I
asked Gregor, because he was still stuck beside me
like glue, completely preventing any interchange
with Ross.

I'd tried at dinner to talk with Ross. . . .

"How long will you be here? I've got the darkroom set up, and John and I want you to come for
dinner."

Before Ross could answer, Gregor leaned forward. "Fran, you can't be so selfish! We're *all* anxious to hear about Mr. Elvig's trip. . . ."

Ross said nothing. His eyes seemed fixed on the
opposite table, and he looked puzzled. It was a
"Where-have-I-seen-you-before?" sort of glance,
which, frankly, I attributed to madame Iandouros;

there was certainly quite a lot of her to be seen. I babbled something to Gregor about "Of course. We'll make it a party, and Ross can tell us about native beauties. . . ."

"What?" said Ross. "Oh—guess you'll have to read it in *Life*. I'm getting out of here tomorrow." But his face had gone sharp with concentration, and despite Gregor's most expert probing, he refused to be drawn out about his trip.

During the stormy piano introduction of "Dich teure Halle" my evening purse slid to the floor. The thing fell open, of course, and Ross poked me gently as he bent to retrieve it. Unconsciously, I bent forward too. Gregor was still absorbed in the music, and as Ross stuffed things back into the bag, I clearly caught "Gotta see you—back gate— soonest!"

Then he'd swept the purse into his hand and returned it to me. I nodded graciously and settled back—but as my eyes slid blandly toward the piano, they encountered monsieur Drouet's dark gaze. After discovering that he spoke perfect English, I had a fanciful idea that perhaps he could read lips, as well. . . .

Eventually, Montalva stopped singing. The servants offered coffee and liqueurs, and the accompanist switched to a gentle doodle of dance tunes. The hard core of bridge players went away to the card tables, and Sir Percival was still present. He'd got Montalva beside him, of course, and was engaged in a delicate flirtation, judging by her full-throated Tuscan chuckles.

Ross drifted off to dance with Sheila, and after one duty dance, Gregor vanished in the same direction. I'd already realized there was a definite undercurrent to the evening, and I was dying to get out to the garden to find out what in hell was going on. Meanwhile, I danced with whoever asked, keeping an eye on Ross's tubby figure. Suddenly I realized that he'd gone—so this was The Moment. I excused myself and made for the ladies' room—and madame Drouet cornered me at once.

"But 'e is *charmant*, your American."

"Who, *Ross?*" I said incredulously. "He's just a magazine photographer I met on a plane." And as she opened her mouth, I added, "And I don't think he knows anything about stamps, either."

She eyed me fleetingly over the edge of her gold compact and snapped it shut with a click. "*Enfin*, he is *amusant*. I hear 'e 'as been in the desert," she said. "Bring him to see me before 'e leave, *hein?*"

"With pleasure, but he's going tomorrow."

"Ah?" She sighed. "It is always the way with one's friends, is it not? They come, and they go. . . ." I said nothing, and she sailed past me into the hall, where Sir Percival at long last was taking formal departure. The Drouets and the rest of the older group followed immediately, in a flurry of bows and "*Merci infiniment!*"

John was playing bridge with madame Iandouros, keeping his eyes on his cards, since he does not care for quite so much display of bosom in public. In the other room, the pianist had had a couple of drinks and was really swinging. I faded rapidly backward to the garden.

Mercifully, it was deserted, and I delicately picked my way around to the back gate that was standard equipment for all our gardens. It always led to an alley for the cars, and on the other side would be the servants' quarters. I could hear snatches of native music and Arabic laughter, and the noise of motors and car doors as the chauffeurs brought out the autos for departing guests. Arab chauffeurs always drive a motor car with as much *pezaz* as they do a camel—but I was glad of the extra din.

There was no sign of Ross, and I felt disconcerted. For a moment I wondered if I'd misunderstood. Had he meant our own back garden gate? Without thinking, I released the catch, meaning to take a cautious peek onto the alley—but the gate swung toward me inexorably.

In the dimness, I could see a dark mass pressed against the gate. With the slow motion of a nightmare, it toppled sideways against me and collapsed on the ground. Simultaneously, the headlights of a car in the alley were switched on, illuminating the scene with cruel clarity.

At my feet lay Ross Elvig—and there was a knife buried to the hilt in his back!

3

I know now that time suspends itself in a crisis, but the mind continues to absorb minute details while the body acts. Hours later I realized that what had seemed an age to me had been no more than one chorus of "That Old Black Magic."

As the headlights in the alley swung across and retreated into darkness, Ross's eyes stared up at me, and with a half-thought that he might yet be alive, I knelt down and said urgently, "Ross, it's Fran. What happened; who . . ."

His hand was still warm in mine, but as my fingers moved to loosen his collar, they slid over a sharp pointed and terrifying moisture. Of its own volition, my body recoiled, and I heard myself screaming like a steam calliope. The music stopped with a crashing discord, and the garden lights flashed on in a confused babble of voices and hurrying feet. Finally I found John's arms about me, and I subsided into tears.

"Shhh, honey—go with signora Francia," he said, and added compellingly in my ear, *"Don't say a word—understand!"*

It was Montalva who saved me. Every time anyone even tried to ask a question, she erupted in floods of indignant Tuscan maternity. "*Ma, questa!* Leave 'er alone, *pòvera bambina!*" She mopped my tears, cuddling me against her generous breasts and crooning, "*Non gridis così cara.* Shh." Somehow she got everyone out of the room . . . and sang me a lullaby!

Eventually, she helped me down the stairs and delivered me to Ibrahim, who took one look at my face and said in an undertone, "I thought it best to come for you myself, madam. Mr. Kennett is . . . occupied."

I knew the grapevine was working overtime when Fatuoma met me at our front door and, without a glance at the ominous smears on my dress, led me upstairs to bed. Usually, even the slightest spot on my clothes and Fatuoma practically made a federal case of it. Tonight, she stripped off the dress and bore it away in silence, returning to hand me a glass of water and an odd-shaped bright blue pellet.

"What's this?" I asked, suspiciously.

"Good," she said. "Sleeeeep!"

"No; I never take sleeping pills," I said, pushing it away.

But she merely shook her head with the effect of stamping a foot and repeated authoritatively, "Dreeeenk!"

I drank.

So it was the following morning before I had a chance to talk with John. He came in with coffee, his eyes looking like burned-out coals, his face gray with exhaustion, and said, "Thank God you're awake; we haven't much time. Alfani's camped downstairs—he's security for the Italians—and Baker's due back any moment, bringing our man with him. It's just courtesy that Alfani's waiting for them."

"Damn Fatuoma, she would make me take a sleeping pill," I said crossly. "I wanted to stay awake."

"Never mind—*what happened?*"

"Ross wanted to tell me something. He whispered to meet him at the back gate," I said, shivering at the memory. "He wasn't in the garden, so I opened the back gate—"

"All right; don't think about it," John said hastily. But I was weeping again, burrowing against his shoulder.

"It was *horrible*. I didn't really like him very well, John, but . . . you know?"

"Yes; I know," he said absently, holding me tightly. "What could he have wanted to tell you, Fran?"

"That's the worst of it. I haven't any idea."

"There must have been something. Tell me exactly what happened, from the top."

I took a long swallow of coffee and tried to collect myself. "Well, I was surprised to see him in the first place," I began. "Did you know he was a guest at the Italian Embassy?" John shook his head wordlessly. "Well, he was—and he said he'd just arrived. But don't you remember, Ibrahim told me he'd seen Ross in the bazaar yesterday morning?"

John's lips tightened. "That's helpful," he said. "I may as well tell you, Fran, they're going to say it was a native who resented Elvig's attentions to a girl."

Without thinking, I scoffed, "Oh, piffle! I don't believe a word of it, John. Ross may not have been quite our sort—he was used to knocking about the world, and he probably used anything to get a good story—but he was perfectly *decent*."

"Perhaps," John said quietly. "But Fran—that's the story; understand?"

"The contract?" I asked, but John's face was blank. "I'm sorry, darling, but I never had a chance to talk with Ross. At dinner, Gregor was right beside me; then there was the concert—I dropped my bag, and that was when Ross whispered to meet him. Later he danced with people. It was only when I saw he'd disappeared that I tried to get out to the garden."

"I see. Listen, honey—there'll be all kinds of questions from all sorts of people, aside from the official bit with Alfani. Can you tell a straight story?"

"Of course."

"Then it's this: You felt in need of fresh air, you went out to the garden, you heard a noise at the back gate and automatically unlatched the thing . . . and Ross's body fell in on you. You screamed, everyone came running, and that's *all* you know. Can you remember that?"

"Of course," I said again, "but what's the real story?"

"God knows," he said wearily. "I wish you could remember something else, but perhaps it's as well you can't. It'll be easier to stick to the story." He leaned back, closing his eyes, while I took another long swallow of scalding coffee and shook myself awake.

"There was something else," I remembered. "It was just an impression—but I thought he recognized someone at the next table during dinner."

John's eyes flew open. "Which table?"

"Drouet, Iandouros Tomyienkov, and . . . Bobby Machlin . . ." I narrowed my eyes and thought back with an effort. The tables had been round, seating fourteen at each. "I can't recall . . . except Sheila. . . ."

"*Sheila!*" John's face went expressionless. "Are you sure?"

"Yes; she was between Tomyienkov and Drouet, almost directly opposite me—and Ian was between madame Iandouros and that Venezuelan girl. . . ."

"And Elvig recognized which one?"

"I don't know," I said miserably, "and I could be wrong. It was just . . . an impression, I tell you. He sort of stared at the table and lost the thread of the conversation, and it was after that— during the concert—that he said to meet him."

"Didn't he dance with you?"

I shook my head. "He tried, but Gregor insisted the first dance was his because he was my dinner partner. . . . And that's another funny thing," I said suddenly.

"What?"

"Gregor. He stuck to me like Scotch Tape every single minute, until Ross was dancing with other people—and *then* he went off to dance with Sheila. It was almost as though he were determined to prevent my having even a word with Ross. And the Tomyienkovs were at that table. John, could that be it, do you think?"

"Perhaps."

I closed my eyes and concentrated once more. "He danced with that Venezuelan girl—what the hell *is* her name, I can never remember it—and signora Francia, and some of the Scandinavian wives, and Sheila. . . ."

"What the devil difference does it make who he danced with?" John said with a strange harshness, and stood up. "You'd better get dressed. Baker and Tom Gerson will be here any moment."

The official questioning was not, after all, too frightening. We sat in the garden with the inevitable pot of Arabian coffee. I was surrounded by three protective American men—and there is nothing any sensible woman would rather be surrounded by—and I spoke my piece with a number of unsimulated shudders. When Alfani seemed inclined to insinuate I might know or suspect a bit more than I was telling (because Mr. Elvig had been my very good friend, after all) I neatly slid out from under.

"Not nearly so good as His Excellency and signora Francia," I pointed out innocently. "*We* didn't know him well enough to have him as a house guest."

"He was not exactly a friend of the Ambassador, either," Alfani stated swiftly. "Merely, he had once photographed our embassy in Athens, and being known to His Excellency . . . and because of the party . . . and I believe he was also known to signorina Montalva. In the diplomatic world, you know how it is—one moves about the world; one meets people over and over again without precisely being *friends*."

I agreed that this was entirely possible. But I had shut him up—and for that I got an approving glance from Mr. Baker. John simply looked *tall*, and shortly afterward Alfani took his leave in a cloud of formal regrets for the unfortunate incident. I could well believe he was worried that an American citizen should have met a sticky end on Italian diplomatic territory!

Mr. Baker accompanied Alfani, but our security officer stayed behind, and as soon as the front door closed, he and John turned to me with a barrage of questions.

"Look," I said finally, banging my hand on the table to silence them. "I've told you and told you—I'll tell you once more from the beginning; then you will go away and sort it out and *leave me alone!*"

"Of course, Mrs. Kennett—but you do understand it's vital to have everything you know?

Sorry to put you through this. I know it was a horrifying experience, but even a word or a look might be helpful."

"Yes, I know, and I'm trying to help, but I've told you everything I can think of except the color of his tie," I said wearily. "So let me begin at the beginning for the *last* time, and will you please *listen* so I don't have to do it again!

"Ross was sitting next to me on the plane. We got to talking; he said he was a commercial photographer on assignment for a magazine and it was one of the most intriguing jobs he'd had recently. I told him I was an amateur photographer; he talked about some of the places he'd visited and various jobs he'd done. . . . As far as I was concerned, he was simply the man in the next seat, and if you're flying five thousand miles, you talk to the person next to you. When we got to Qeman, I said, 'It's been nice talking to you,' and expected to leave it there. But he . . . sort of attached himself to me, because I was a photographer."

I repeated everything Ross had said the day he met me after marketing and everything I could recall of the previous evening. Nothing seemed to strike a responsive chord, and I had only one small suggestion to add. "Alfani said the Francias knew him only because he'd photographed the embassy in Athens," I reminded them. "Madame Iandouros was at that table. Could it possibly have been she?"

"God knows, if it was," John said involuntarily, "he couldn't possibly have failed to recognize her.

No matter how he knew her, that dress left nothing in doubt."

"Well, that's absolutely all I can tell you," I returned firmly. "Now, you go off and play around with it. I'm tired."

Presumably they did, but to no avail. The official story, as John had said, was that Ross had been killed by a native over an Arab girl. The body was shipped home; there was a formal note from the Italian Embassy to the American Embassy, expressing regret that such an incident should have occurred in their diplomatic bailiwick, and subsequently—silence. Not even madame Drouet ever mentioned "my American," and since she was usually neither to hold nor to bind about anything, that in itself was significant.

I couldn't dismiss it so easily. For days I felt sad that I hadn't, somehow, been able to help. If only I'd reached the back gate sooner . . . or if I could guess what Ross had wanted to tell me. I worried each scrap of memory like a dog with a bone and ended with nothing except a conviction that the murder was tied in with the oil contract. It could only be that, and I wondered whether the editors of *Life* had been able to help. If they explained exactly what Ross's assignment was, it might furnish a lead to whatever he'd stumbled on. Vaguely, I wondered also what had become of his photographic equipment and the films he'd wanted me to process.

I couldn't ask. Not even John. The one time I tried, he actually snapped at me, "I told you to leave it to the authorities . . . and will you *stop* fussing over who he recognized. You admit yourself he didn't ask about anyone at the other table. It's all in your mind, and if you persist in trying to involve them, you'll only stir up worse trouble than there is already."

I forgave his annoyance on the score that the oil contract was upsetting. He and Mr. Baker were working early and late, even doing all the typing themselves—and yet, by the week before the Feast of Ramadan, the spy had ferreted out everything but the actual contract provisions, and there were rumblings of discontent among the natives.

"Why not tell them the facts, so they can see they aren't being rooked?"

"Not now." John shook his head. "We never expected it to take so long, but now we can't hope to finalize in a week—and they won't sign anything or even discuss business during Ramadan. If the present status were known in detail, there'd be a month for someone to work out a better deal."

"I thought you said these concessions were standard."

"Only the general provisions. There's no fixed financial arrangement. Each concession is negotiated individually, and everyone makes the best deal he can. You know how Easterns love bargaining, Fran. Aside from the actual royalty of so many cents per barrel of oil, they want all sorts of other things. They ask for an exhorbitant royalty, we offer a very small one; they say they'll take less if we'll build them a school, and we come up a

few cents and say they can have a playground—
and so on.

"The thing fluctuates from day to day," he finished grimly, "depending on government finances
and the way they happen to feel. To do him justice, this Sheikh is trying to get the most he can
for his people. It's his first big chance, and he's
determined to make the most of it. We thrash out
one point, and while we're writing it into the contract, he's busy thinking up something new to toss
at us tomorrow."

"How infuriating!"

"You'd die to hear some of the things he's asked
for—like a kid, seeing how far he can go before
you smack him." John snorted wearily. "He even
wanted three grand pianos for his wives."

"Only three?"

"That's what Baker asked, and His Highness
said three would be enough because he always
keeps a wife-position open, in case he has to marry
a nomad's daughter to prevent trouble in the desert," John explained, poker-faced. "He divorces
wife number one just before the wedding, so there
would always be a piano free."

"Good heavens; it sounds like the Mad Hatter's
tea party!"

"It's all of that and more, but exactly the way
old ibn-Saud kept control. This lad is just as smart.
The trouble is, he wants everything ever written
into *any* oil contract, except the Kuwaiti's gold
yacht. Since Qeman hasn't a seaport, he'll settle
for a gold airplane."

"With diamond controls?"

"Shhh, don't give him any ideas! Oh, he's amenable in a way, but from his point of view, one corporation is the same as another—they're all foreign and fair game. So you can see, Fran, if it were known exactly what we're offering, someone could come up with a bit extra—and he'd take it with no hesitation. Can't blame him, but that's why we have to play it this way." John was silent for a moment, biting his lips. "The hell of it is," he burst out, "we can't put our finger on the troublemaker. It can't be anyone in the palace or the government—they'd already *know* how far we've gotten toward agreement. There'd be no need of native unrest; that's only to smoke us out, because they don't know what extra to offer. His Highness is ethical—he's not playing us against another group. If he had any clue to identify who wants to outbid us, he'd say so. He's as disturbed as we are, equally anxious for secrecy—but the country comes first. He'll break off negotiations entirely, rather than have an uprising. He's said as much— but we've got too much time and money in this already to put it off for, maybe, another year.

"The leak is somewhere outside the palace," he went on, "but damned if we can find it. I'm thinking of sending you up to Lebanon for a month, Fran, until Ramadan is over and we know how serious the local situation may be."

I looked at his sober face and felt my heart bump painfully. I'd always wondered, academically, what I'd do if I thought John were in danger. Now I knew. "You can stop thinking. I'm not interested in safety without you. I won't go."

His face was strangely sad as he kissed me. "I was afraid you'd say that. I'm only trying to spare you unhappiness, but I won't insist."

Unhappiness? It was a peculiar word to have used. Surely *danger* would have been more accurate—or would it? Now that I'd obediently pushed Ross Elvig into a mental closet and shut the door, I suddenly realized that despite John's heavy work schedule, he was still finding time for Sheila.

It was borne in on me most subtly, not in words but by the absence of them—by discreet silences and tactfully averted eyes when John and Sheila danced together. Most of all, by the change in Ian Haysrath, who was still showing up for tea and drinking it iced. He'd abandoned all flirtation, and when he made a complimentary remark, it was sincere. I couldn't really like him, but when he was talking simply, he could be good company. He had all the wicked understated humor of the English and a gift for hilarious reminiscences of past stations.

Nevertheless, I felt an odd gentleness when we were together, and at the nightly parties (which are all that a foreign colony has for amusement in a small country), he drank a bit less and danced with me a bit more—usually at the other side of the room from John and Sheila. In the end I was left in no doubt of his, and the general, opinion of the relationship between my husband and his wife.

My initial reaction was repudiation, total disbelief. As I've said, John seems born to be a movie actor with a zillion females sighing over his picture; instead, he's a mining engineer. Do not ask me how I got him. After five years of marriage, I merely accept my good fortune as one accepts the existence of the universe. I am not smug, but John is not the type that wants an adoring doormat for a wife. In general, he dislikes feminine coquetry; it interferes with his career, which basically absorbs him. I have sometimes thought that explained his marriage. A wife automatically prevents misconstructions, and with anything that looks like John, the merest pleasantry of social intercourse could swiftly (and hopefully) be interpreted as an invitation to quite another sort.

We'd had a few incidents but nothing I couldn't handle tactfully. I doubt whether he ever even knew about the consul's teenage daughter in Somaliland. He had been concentrating on a seismograph survey, which had naturally filled his mind to the exclusion of female hysteria. And once I had pointed out the need for a college-educated wife who could keep pace with John's brilliance, she had returned to Mount Holyoke, fired with determination to rise and shine. I heard later she made Phi Beta Kappa in her junior year, and later still she married a dentist. Annually, I get Christmas cards from her thankful mother.

Privately I've thought it part of my good fortune that John has a single-track mind. Like the Boston ladies who "have their hats," John *has* a wife for all requirements aside from his beloved job. I am not smug about his fidelity either—he is merely too busy for romantic dalliance, and since luckily, I proved satisfactory for his lighter moments, why look farther?

Now, in the heat of Qeman, I wasn't so sure. As he'd said, this foreign colony was different. Quite apart from the undercurrent over the contract, it was the first place I'd encountered serious glances and silence. Was it merely a more sophisticated colony, so used to *affaires* that it assumed a situation where none existed? Or for the first time was John really aware of another woman?

The best cure for a problem is work. I got out my photographic equipment and got the darkroom set up, sternly suppressing the memory of Ross Elvig. Ibrahim had Fouad build shelves and got someone to run a cord into the deep closet for the processing light and someone else to construct a sink with a water tap. I dug out the films I'd brought from Toledo and went to work. In the dim silence of the darkroom, thought was possible, and a number of things came back to me.

Madame Drouet: "It was time you came—it is not good to leave a husband for long in these hot climates."

Sheila Haysrath: "You're one of the lucky ones. . . . John knows, I've cried all over him a couple of times."

Ian's unobtrusive protectiveness . . . the swiftly changed conversations when I entered a cloakroom . . . John's shock, his shutting me up and forbidding mention of Ross's interest in the table that held Sheila . . .

Always before, there had been only kindly amusement among adults in a colony over the girls who lost their hearts to John—who couldn't remember their names, never noticed the heartburnings and the machinations to get a seat beside him. Occasionally there were married women who were obviously open to suggestion; John avoided them, if they managed to get the suggestion across to him in the first place.

Qeman was different. Sliding negatives from one pan to another, I remembered that he hadn't really wanted me to join him. Oh, he hadn't said in so many words, "Don't come; I don't want you," but his letters had been increasingly offputting: It was only an interim post, lousy climate, why not stay comfortably home until he was reassigned, wouldn't be long. . . . Off-putting to the point that some sixth sense had led me to pack up and merely wire time of arrival. I'd thought it was probably a minor annoyance, like bad food or poor quarters—something he wanted to spare me. But I had been secretly convinced that if I were there, he'd be glad to have me.

Was he?

Certainly, he had greeted me affectionately—but now I recalled the lack of expression on his face as I'd seen it from the plane window while we were landing, and his unaccustomed taciturnity in these past weeks. Usually John told me *everything*, often rather more than I wished to hear, but his only reservation would be business details. Now he was disclosing the business but oddly silent on the general gossip. I was still completely his wife, even if his weariness made it less frequent than usual, but this meant he wasn't over the line with Sheila Haysrath. Not yet. If I hadn't turned up when I did, perhaps . . . but you can't live with and love a man for five years without knowing him more intimately than his superficial actions.

John is not a two-timer. If he could make love to me, I was solo, no matter what the colony suspected. So I'd arrived in time to prevent adultery, but there's more to marriage than who's in the bed. For a woman like me, mental fidelity is the important thing. If John were being torn between his legal tie to me and a growing desire for Sheila, I wouldn't want to hold him.

I'll admit I strongly doubted that Sheila could seriously capture John's affections—he'd had much more attractive chances—but when I examined it carefully (trying to be objective and non-egotistical), I decided it was possible. I had always tried to be self-reliant, to cope with anything and everything so John needn't be disturbed. Perhaps I'd overdone it. He'd said, "Sometimes you can be so uncompromising, Fran." Maybe he found Sheila's ineptitudes appealing, a refreshing change from competence. He's always been all male, instinctively protective—and he never gave a damn what he ate, so long as it was edible and there was enough of it.

Sheila was blond; John liked blonds. She was closer to him in age than I—John is ten years older than my twenty-six; Sheila was thirty-four. She'd already been all over the world; I'd only gone where John had. And I might think she was a miserable housekeeper, but perhaps she'd do better for a husband who gave her a word of praise now and then.

I fought down instinctive inner jeering at the concept of Sheila Haysrath's ever being anything but a pallid slob, and ended with "Wait and see," which is probably how all wives temporize in similar situations. I was staring dully into darkness, when there was a tap on the darkroom door. "Yes?"

"Telephone, madam—madame Iandouros. You can answer?" It was Fouad's voice. I slid from the stool and abandoned John's possible emotional defection. The prints were drying on the farther shelf. "Yes; I'm coming." I left the darkroom and went to the phone in the morning room, hearing the soft click of the main telephone being replaced when I said, *"Bonjour, madame. Comment vous portez-vous aujourd'hui?"* It took a full fifteen minutes of politesse in the slow, laborious French that was the only way she and I could communicate, before it was settled that we would be *"comble d'honneur"* to attend a small party next Thursday, in honor of someone with an un-

pronounceable Greek name. I noted it on the en-
gagement pad, knowing full well there'd be no
conflict—but if you don't carefully put down
where you are supposed to go, you may easily
wind up at the Turks' instead of the Mexicans'. I'd
learned that the hard way, when we'd come in
from the out country to Nairobi—and only got to
the proper party by following the limousine
traffic. At the time, John had thought it the best
joke of the year, but we hadn't been married very
long.

Tonight, according to the calendar, was "informal at the Portuguese's." It was nearly six, and I
wondered vaguely that Ian hadn't shown up at
four-thirty, as usual. Perhaps he was out of Qeman. In view of my cogitations during the afternoon, I was as well pleased. I wasn't too sure what
I meant to do—if anything—but it would be easier
without Ian. I got up from the telephone desk and
went to my bedroom, to find it dark and silent,
the shutters tight-closed against the cruel late-
afternoon sun of Qeman. For a moment, I was surprised to find no sign of Fatuoma, running my
bath, making ready for the evening, but probably
she had not expected me quite so early.

Automatically, I flipped the light switch—and
suppressed a scream.

Fatuoma lay crumpled on the floor, my purple
dinner dress flowing over her. Beyond, the darkroom door was swinging open. . . .

4

She was alive, and her pulse was fairly strong and even (as much as I could recall of first-aid courses). I took a swift glance into the darkroom, and it was a mess—the floor a sludge of overset pans; negatives and prints gone. I closed the door and switched on lamps, and Fatuoma was stirring, moaning faintly. I knelt beside her, but I could see no sign of blood. She'd apparently been knocked out and was already coming to. I turned off the glaring overhead light, soaked a washcloth in cool water, and sped back to bathe her forehead. Suddenly her eyes fluttered briefly, opened, and stared up at me.

"Fatuoma, what happened—who was here?" I whispered urgently.

Her hand writhed convulsively, twisting snake-like to grasp mine. "Not know," she murmured painfully. "Come to make ready, press button for light, go to closet for dress, and when come out"— her eyes shadowed in remembered fright—"is small noise. I begin turn—is all I know."

"Shhh; it's all right," I soothed, stroking her hand gently. "I'm afraid we had a thief."

Fatuoma's eyes flickered again, and she struggled to sit up, moaning slightly while I slid my arm about her. "He not get pretty pearls?" she asked anxiously.

"No, no," I assured her, suppressing tears at her concern for my paltry gems—a double strand of pink pearls John had got ("Never ask me how!") in Dutch Timor. "He got nothing; he must have been so disturbed by you that he simply ran away. Oh, Fatuoma, I'm so sorry you were hurt—shall we call the doctor to be certain you're all right?"

"No!" she said sharply. "No, is nothing, not want doctor." She pulled away from me and scrambled to her feet, swaying a little, obviously gritting her teeth to stand erect—but she was adamant in refusing a doctor, and I didn't press her. Natives in any country often distrust medicos. I felt fairly sure she'd merely been tapped on the head while someone made his getaway, and aside from a sore spot, Fatuoma would be all right in a day or two. Better to leave it to her than to publicize the affair—because it could only be part of the spying. I realized that at once—as well as a few other upsetting implications.

I almost literally forced her to lie down on the chaise longue, while I ran my own bath, found fresh underclothing, and quietly got dressed. I think she slept briefly, which is the best possible restorative, but she was groggily on duty by the time I was finished—stumbling about, hunting for the evening purse, scarf, and gloves to accompany my dress. "Thank you, Fatuoma. You are off duty as of this minute," I said, holding her eyes compellingly. "You understand? You are to go to your room and to bed at once. If I see you again before tomorrow, I shall be angry. You understand?"

"Yes." She twisted her hands together. "Ibrahim not like."

"I'll take care of Ibrahim."

She nodded, but I wasn't sure she even heard me any longer. Poor kid, she was going through the automatic motions of clearing up, practically falling flat on her face every time she bent over. If I could have got my hands on whoever punched her, right that moment, I'd have punched him into next week! "Leave everything—go to bed *now*," I said gently, turning her to the door with me.

She was inclined to protest; Ibrahim would disapprove if all were not tidy when he made his inspection, and she might lose her job.

"Over my dead body," I assured her grimly, wondering how much she was paying him for it—but if I had to pay him myself, I wasn't about to lose Fatuoma. It was not merely that she was a superb maid, but she had been clobbered instead of me.

I'd figured that out while I was sloshing in the bathtub. If I'd finished the phone call two minutes earlier—if Fatuoma had been two minutes later—it would have been I who came prancing back to the darkroom closet, to encounter an interloper and be knocked cold. In a way it was better that Fatuoma had got the clout; if she had found *me* on the floor, the entire household would have been roused, and by now the rest of the colony would have been tuned in.

Anyone who has experienced life abroad finds it incredible that radio had to be *invented*.

The intruder also had to be someone attached to our household. Not necessarily one of our own servants, who would certainly have been gone over with a fine-tooth comb before being hired to staff a household engaged in critical negotiations, but some one of the hangers-on who cluster about the kitchen quarters in any Eastern country. One grows accustomed to semisupporting all the relatives of one's servants, to discovering half a dozen scantily clad small children playing ball in the garage court, or encountering a placid octogenarian sitting in the sunny spot beside the rear gate. One asks polite questions, leading to formal introductions, and one mentally chalks up six, eight, or ten extra rice bowls. I have never determined how they arrive at the precise quota that is the maximum without breaking the camel's back, but I have learned that the more extra rice bowls, the greater "face" and the better the service. But rice is cheap by American standards, and it pays off handsomely, in the form of expert mending and delicate cabinet work, and the kids are always overjoyed to be entrusted with small errands.

But no child had knocked out Fatuoma. Futhermore, it was not only someone she'd have recognized, but someone who she'd have known had no business in madam's rooms. That argued that it hadn't been one of our servants; any one of them

could have given *some* explanation for his presence. Even Selim, the chauffeur, could have said
he was looking for me to get his instructions for
the evening, and naturally he'd blundered into the
wrong spot, since he rarely ever came upstairs.

No—whether or not it was a servant, it was
someone close enough to our staff to know I'd
spent the day processing film and had been called
away to a phone call. It was also someone who
knew the house well enough to seize the chance of
getting my negatives and prints, and someone
who wanted *only* those, only what I'd been working on this first day I had used the darkroom.
There was no way to pinpoint any particular person; what one knew, all would know in two minutes, and the upper gallery outside the bedrooms
made it possible to get into my room without
going through the house.

What in heaven's name could anyone think I'd
have that was worth such a daring theft? The condition of the darkroom attested flurry, haste to the
exclusion of concealment. I'd closed the door on
the mess, but it was vivid in my mind. Someone
had dashed in, seized every bit of paper in evidence, scooped up drying prints and wet negatives,
overturning pans recklessly—and been trapped by
Fatuoma, coming a few minutes early to lay out
my clothes for the evening.

It had been a man, of course; Fatuoma would
not have questioned any of the women servants,
nor could one of them have knocked her out. I
thought drily that whoever it was would be flum-

moxed to discover the photographic record of a backyard barbecue in Toledo, Ohio.

I knew the answer, naturally. I couldn't prove it any more than I could prove that Ross Elvig had recognized someone at the other dinner table before he was killed, but it was clear in my mind. What Fatuoma's attacker had wanted, hoped, expected to get were prints of Ross's films.

Slowly descending the stairs to our front hall, I saw Ibrahim in his usual place, impassive, immaculately white-robed, waiting to open the door and politely bow me away to the evening's entertainment. It struck me that the one person who might suspect I had Ross Elvig's films would be Ibrahim.

He'd been in the car the morning Ross had declared himself in for coffee. He understood English perfectly. He not only knew the darkroom, but had provided the workmen for constructing it. And Ibrahim always answered the telephone. He would know that any conversation between Mrs. Kennett and madame Iandouros would take considerable time because of inexpert French.

I looked down at his impersonal face, staring into space expressionlessly. I knew he was perfectly aware of my halt, halfway down the stairs, though not a muscle quivered. Deliberately I stood still, drawing on evening gloves and surveying him—and I couldn't for a single instant visualize Ibrahim racing around collecting prints and negatives. He was still the only member of our staff who would have known everything and fitted all of it together and who could have dispatched an underling who would unquestioningly carry out his orders. If so, he must already be aware that the job was bungled and that Fatuoma had had to be silenced. Did he know it was wasted effort? I wondered what he'd make out of the backyard in Toledo?

Calmly I continued to the lower hall. "Ibrahim, Fatuoma is not feeling well. I have sent her to bed. Please see that she is not disturbed."

"Certainly, madam." If I'd expected any reaction, I was disappointed. Ibrahim swung open the door, followed me down the path, and assisted me into the car behind Selim. "Enjoy your evening, madam," he said formally, and cast a word that was presumably Arabic for "Portuguese" to Selim, who grinned broadly, nodding his head. The door closed quietly, and the car moved forward, smoothly heading for the Portuguese Embassy. Glancing aside, I could see Ibrahim's white robes billowing about him as he strode rapidly back to the house. Going to find out what had happened?

One peculiar thing about marriage is the difficulty of telling anything to your husband when you want to. Something is always in the way—like tonight's party. It was a total disaster in more ways than one. John was overtired to begin with and should have been home in bed with a bowl of soup, instead of smiling at the same people he'd seen last night and would see again tomorrow. Somebody clumsily dropped a dinner plate upsidedown on the carpet—although after a few bites of my own dinner, I was tempted to follow suit—and Ian got filthy drunk for the first time in several weeks.

By the time we got home, John was looking white around the gills and somewhat shorter than usual. I'd had time for second thoughts, which were principally that whatever I suspected, no matter how logical it appeared to me, I still had no shred of proof. I might be convinced that whoever had conked Fatuoma and upset my darkroom had hoped to get Ross Elvig's films—but that only implied that someone wasn't sure what had become of them. I knew I didn't have them; in fact, I'd have expected them to be in the hands of our security man, Gerson—or perhaps already mailed to *Life* before Ross was killed.

And in the last analysis, why would anyone think *I* had the things? Only Ibrahim, who'd overheard Ross pressing me to set up the darkroom. But why would he think I'd wait so long before processing?

Looking at John's exhausted face as he crawled into bed, and remembering Ian's foul behavior this evening, I couldn't raise a new problem. John kissed me rather haphazardly, flumped onto his side with a groan, and was asleep before I'd turned out the light.

I lay awake for a while, pondering what best to do. Tell Gerson, if I got a chance; continue the fiction of a sneak thief for Fatuoma's benefit—and quietly clear up the darkroom mess as soon as John left tomorrow morning.

Early as it was when I'd finished my first cup of coffee, brought by a woman I vaguely identified as the cook's wife, someone had been before me. The instant the woman was gone, I slid out of bed and threw open the darkroom door.

It was as pristine as though I had never used it.

More food for thought, although the explanation was obvious—Ibrahim had got the details from Fatuoma and had either cleaned up personally or stood over another servant until all trace of the thief was gone. I chalked up a plus for Ibrahim—not that I'd ever underestimated his intelligence, but if there'd ever been a fingerprint anywhere in that closet, it wasn't there now. I couldn't ask, even when he met me at the foot of the stairs later, with such perfect timing that I knew he'd been lying in wait, and said, "Good morning, Mrs. Kennett. I regret you did not ring. I took the liberty of sending Fatuoma home to rest, but Noami is ready to serve you. I apologize for the inconvenience."

"Thank you, Ibrahim, but I've been dressing and undressing myself for twenty-odd years," I returned sweetly, "so it's really no hardship. If you will ask Noami to press the yellow printed cocktail dress and jacket for tonight. I've no doubt we shall go on very well until Fatuoma feels able to return."

Once again, I thought I saw the beginnings of a smile in Ibrahim's eyes, but he only bowed and handed me the morning's telephone messages. They'd been placed by servants, of course; no one in Qeman made a personal phone call before eleven A.M.—not even Berthe Drouet, who generally took pleasure in flouting custom. "At my age, it is not merely the morning face that is unrecognizable. The voice, too, is—'ow you say?—weird!" She pronounced it in two distinct syllables: We, and eared, but by now I wouldn't have corrected her, even if I'd been cursed with an earnest mentality.

Neither would I have trusted Berthe Drouet any farther than I could push the Rock of Gilbraltar with my nose, if it came to diplomacy or any least upset for Henri. But for sheer friendliness in every other department, and for entertainment value, she was the joy of my life. Henri had not "emerged" since the night of Ross Elvig's murder, but madame Drouet had attended every party, escorted by one or another of the French attachés, who quite evidently considered it no hardship to beau the boss's wife. Apparently, she was funny in English but even more amusing in French, judging by their delighted chuckles.

All the same, she had a tapir's nose for news. If anyone in Qeman had learned of Fatuoma's accident, Berthe Drouet would be first. I looked at the phone slip. "Madame Drouet requests madame Kennett to phone." Over a cigarette, I worked out a story: Fatuoma had turned her ankle in a splash of water on the tile floor while preparing my bath, had fallen against the edge of the tub and knocked herself out. I had found her when I returned from speaking with madame Iandouros, and Ibrahim had sent her home to rest for a day and provided a substitute to bridge the gap until Fatuoma returned. That ought to answer all questions.

I pulled the telephone toward me and got through to the French Embassy, only to find that madame Drouet had no questions. She merely wished to pass the time of day, to discuss the disaster at the Portuguese's last night, to speculate maliciously on what might be anticipated at the Brazilians' tonight. When finally I'd rung off, I felt fairly certain the whole incident was a closed book—and I was more than ever convinced that Ibrahim was involved, for he was the only person with sufficient authority to be able to seal the mouths of the staff to the point that no word had got out.

In fact, it argued an even higher degree of autocracy than I'd dreamed. Anyone who can totally suppress native gossip is A Personage, and one to be reckoned with. I was happier than ever that I hadn't told John, because he is inclined to forget diplomacy in favor of "getting to the bottom of things." As matters stood, nobody was anywhere, and hooray for the home team. I'd lost my vacation pictures, was all. Mother would be disappointed when I said there was a defect in the camera and none of the pix had come out. John would never ask at all, particularly with everything else on his mind.

Fatuoma returned next day, looking entirely recovered and kissing my hand for not deducting from her wages for the absence. When I probed a bit, she only shrugged philosophically. "Is thief, many we have in Qeman. Police not catch, you not worry, Ibrahim say he take care."

I let it go at that, and gladly, because what we did *not* need at this moment was An Incident. The Feast of Ramadan is the most serious and religious of holidays. All Qeman was preparing for it, but there was an undercurrent of uneasiness. As I went about the shops, I sensed withdrawal. True, the shopkeepers were always inscrutable, but there was an air of faint dislike, of disapproval, that unnerved me. Near the end of the week I thought I felt a pebble thrown at me. I told myself it was gravel scattered by my shoe, but a glance at Ibrahim's face was unsettling.

He caught my eye. "Perhaps you should leave the rest of your purchases to me, Mrs. Kennett." And without waiting for reply, he summoned Selim forward. Somehow, before I quite knew how it had happened, I was in the car and spinning toward home.

Behind the chauffeur's impassive white-clad back, I knew for the first time what it's like to be a pariah. A pebble in a marketplace can so easily become a knife in the dark. . . . In the midst of the cruel heat, I felt cold. "Selim," I said, sharply, "take me to Bêt Americano."

He nodded politely over his shoulder. "Ah-yes'm." That was most of the English he knew, but his broad ebony grin was so normal that I felt ashamed of my fears. The big house Mr. Baker used as both home and office was shaded and reassuring. I hesitated, after all, to disturb John. "I'll wait for Mr. Kennett in the lounge," I told the servant. "Please bring me something cool to drink. Oh," I said casually over my shoulder, "is Mr. Gerson still here?"

The servant shook his head. "He gone Kuwait this morning."

So *that* was no good, and I sat for a long time, sipping lemonade and glancing at magazines, telling myself it was all imagination. But the things that had happened to Ross Elvig and Fatuoma were inescapable facts, even if I didn't have the missing pieces. Eventually, I must have dozed in the quiet coolness of the room. I had no idea of the time when I was startled awake by an angry murmur. The room was shadowed and silent, no lights had been lit, and the insistent humming seemed to come from outside.

Running to the window, I saw a sea of white-clad Arabs flowing before me, shouting, gesticulating, only dimly heard through the sealed windows of the air-conditioned room. Snatching up purse and gloves, I made for the door—and paused. Massed in the hall outside the office doors were Mr. Baker's servants.

All the newspaper stories I'd ever seen of riots in Oriental countries came back to me. With pure reflex action, I slipped out of my pumps and slid along the wall from lounge to stairs, where I crawled up to the second floor as rapidly as possible. I didn't think I'd penetrated the servants' absorption, but it would be only a matter of time before someone remembered admitting Mrs. Kennett.

As I ran frantically through one passage after another, searching for the rear stairs, I could faintly hear Mr. Baker's hearty bass voice exhorting, pleading . . . interspersed with boos and a small explosion. Firecrackers sounded like that; I knew this was not a firecracker. Native feet were ascending the stairs behind me, and still I could not find the servant staircase. It must be behind a door, but I'd got myself into a cul-de-sac that appeared to be nothing *but* doors. Breathlessly, I stepped into a niche and cowered beside one of the florid statues that infested the house. With luck I might be unnoticed, since my dress was nearly the color of wall paint and marble statue . . . or should I step forth boldly and quell the advancing servants by calm demeanor and white supremacy?

To my left, a door opened quietly, cutting off all possibility of flight . . . *and the figure methodically, noiselessly opening the other doors was Ibrahim.* Searching for me, of course. Selim would have said where he'd driven me. Shrinking into the farther corner of the niche, I thought that if he only moved around the bend of the hall, I could make that door. It had to be the rear stairs. For an instant, his attention seemed deflected by the advancing group, but just as I was about to break for it, he turned and saw me.

With incredible speed, Ibrahim stood before me—but not with a menacing knife. Instead, he spread wide his white robes and leaned negligently against the niche in which I trembled, completely blocking me from view with one hand to the wall, one leg crossed, in an attitude of unconcern. There was an interchange in Arabic. Ibrahim's tone, like his pose, was casually indifferent. After a while, the footsteps retreated. Catlike, Ibrahim reconnoitered, then drew back and seized my arm with gentle strength. "Come," he whispered, and eased open the door.

Down we fled, into the deserted kitchens and through a small passageway to a door half-hidden behind cloths and brushes. In swift silence, he rummaged in a basket, drew a soiled sheet from tomorrow's laundry, and draped it skillfully about me, tossing my shoes aside. "Can you walk in stocking feet?" he whispered. At my nod, he said, "Follow a little behind me, and try to take small steps like an Arab woman."

He opened the rear door, and, a silent procession of two, we proceeded across the kitchen court without haste. I remembered the subservient, obsequious mien of the Arab woman and did my best to imitate it. Probably it was the best performance I've ever given, for we strolled calmly through a mob of jostling, screaming, furious Arabs and reached the courtyard of the Russian Embassy, which adjoins ours. In the windows I could see Gregor and the other aides, but Ibrahim hissed, "Do not go in; follow me." With a last glance at the expressionless Russians above, we strode solemnly past, through their shadowy garden and out to the street. Ibrahim looked up and down carefully.

"Quickly!" he commanded, and whisked me into a native carriage whose driver had abandoned it for bigger sport. I tumbled into the back from his vigorous shove, while he swung into the front and urged the decrepit horse forward.

Suddenly, I found my voice. "Stop!" I cried. "Ibrahim, Mr. Kennett . . ."

"They will not do any harm tonight," he said indifferently. "I think you would have been safe, but the servants might have frightened you. A woman is better at home."

We reached our house, and Ibrahim courteously helped me from the carriage. "Perhaps I would have been safe," I said, "but I think you saved my life. Why?"

Contemptuously, he stripped away the soiled sheet and dropped it to the ground. "Americans are not bad, Mrs. Kennett. They do not really exploit us, and we could not exist without the things they give us, too. My brother had an operation in the oil company hospital at Djurdel. A famous surgeon came from Europe, specially for him. Now he sees."

"Oh, Thank you, Ibrahim."

"It is nothing," he said politely. "Go to Fatuoma, while I get word of Mr. Kennett."

I was bathed, cooled, and calmed and had answered five curious telephone inquiries with casual evasiveness before John came in. He put his arms about me silently for a moment. "Fran, darling—Ibrahim told me you were there, upstairs. I never knew—nobody announced you. Are you all right, honey?"

I nodded. "I told them not to disturb you. I was waiting in the lounge, but it all happened so quickly . . . I thought I'd go up and get out through the back stairs before the servants remembered I was there, but I couldn't find the right door, and finally Ibrahim came after me."

"It wasn't really dangerous," John said, "but it could easily have turned from a demonstration to a full-scale riot." He shook his head somberly. "Baker was magnificent. He told them nothing was being done without the consent of the Sheikh, and they knew they could rely on their ruler to protect their interests fully."

I shivered. "I heard a gunshot. You might have been killed."

"Not this time," he said positively. "Last thing they want just before Ramadan, not sure they even wanted a demonstration. You're right it boiled up quickly. We don't know what sparked it. Baker thinks it wasn't meant, but got out of hand. One thing—the local police aren't in it, nor most of the people. They'd simply joined a crowd to see what was up, and the instant the police arrived, it wasn't five minutes before everyone faded away. Perfectly good-humored, chuckling and laughing as though they'd been to a camel race or something!

"Another thing," he went on, "it shows there's a definite plan behind this. It's more than petty spying by someone hoping to make a fast buck. We'd pretty well settled for a servant, shrewd enough to know he could sell the details in a dozen places, purely for curiosity value. Even other oil companies would be interested, without necessarily intending to outbid. But if it were a loner, he'd never let it get to the point of a demonstration. In no time, the bazaar would put a finger on him. The town is mostly loyal. Someone would whisper to a Sheikh's man, and the jig would be up."

"The Russians," I said, and described those silent watchers at the windows of their Embassy.

"Stirring up the nationalist element is a Russian trick, but I don't know . . . it doesn't fit, this time."

"I'll tell you where it does fit—Ross Elvig."

"That again? Now what?" John impatience became appalled concentration when I detailed the attack on Fatuoma. "My God, Fran—why didn't you tell me this?"

"Because you told me to shut up and leave it to the authorities," I countered flatly. "And I can't *prove* anything, John, but what other explanation could there be? For all I know, *Life* already has his films and the spy simply wasn't sure."

"No, *Life* doesn't have the films—at least, they have some, but they can tell there must have been more to complete the assignment. We never found the rest. Alfani searched the Embassy intensively. His cameras were in his room, unloaded. We checked every processor from Basra to Cairo; no one admits receiving them, and there's no reason to question it. This puts a different face on it."

"Well, I meant to tell Gerson, but he's away. I'm only certain of one thing—it isn't Ibrahim, even if he did clean up the evidence and knows more than he's telling."

Oddly, John snorted with amusement. "No, it isn't Ibrahim, and he does know more than he's telling you, darling. In fact, we all do." He hesitated, lighting a cigarette, as though debating with himself. "You'd better know," he decided finally. "He's a distant cousin of the Sheikh, and the reason we have him is at His Highness's request, admittedly to protect the Sheikh's interests."

"But . . . doesn't he tell you anything either?" I gasped.

"Sometimes. He didn't tell me about the darkroom, although I suppose the palace knows about it. I'll have a word with him later."

"You mean you're going to tell *him?*"

"He's as much concerned with our spy as we are, Fran, and much more apt to identify the person. He's our unofficial liaison," John explained.

"Baker was tickled pink that His Highness suggested planting Ibrahim on us. So far it's worked like a charm. Ibrahim's report has demonstrated conclusively that we're hiding nothing, which pays off in increasingly cordial relations and government cooperation. You weren't supposed to know, but if you keep getting involved," he sighed ruefully, "well, your safety is more important than orders. If anything more happens, you can rely on Ibrahim completely. Nothing gets past him."

I absorbed this in silence for a moment. "I'd rather rely on you completely, if you don't mind," I said finally. "And I wouldn't be so sure nothing gets past him."

"What do you mean?"

"When you're having that word with him, suppose you inquire who was regularly and repeatedly searching my rooms for weeks after I first arrived," I replied slowly. "It wasn't Fatuoma—she was as surprised as I was."

John's eyebrows shot up nearly to his hairline. "Why didn't you *tell* me?" he demanded.

"I supposed it was just servant curiosity; it happens in every foreign country." I shrugged, slightly nettled. "And if it comes to that, *I* wish you hadn't told me I've been giving orders to a relative of His Highness."

"It's worse than that," John told me, poker-faced. "He's a Cambridge man."

"England or Massachusetts?" I asked suspiciously.

"Harvard." At my snort for his duplicity, he

added casually, "*Summa cum laude*, Hasty Pudding, class of fifty-five. Hadn't you better dress for dinner?" He'd disappeared into his dressing room before I finished gulping.

Not bad enough to be telling royalty there was a scorpion in the bathroom, and please advise the laundress the napkins weren't clean enough? My steward was as Ivy League as my husband! The humor of it struck me at last. Good God, it could happen only to me! Wait till I told the girls back home that John was so important the Sheikh assigned a relative to attend to our personal comfort. By the time my frivolous mind had worked on that story, I was inwardly convulsed at the probable reaction in Toledo, Ohio. Fatuoma smiled at my subdued chuckles. "Is nice you happy, all safe now." She handed over purse, gloves, and shawl and surveyed me proudly. "Look *very* pretty tonight."

"Thank you, Fatuoma. Don't wait up for me." If I didn't say that, she'd be sitting sleepily on the floor by the bed until we got home, even if it was three in the morning. I went out to the top of the stairs and could see John standing below with Ibrahim.

Everything was exactly as usual—except that now I knew Ibrahim's real position. Did he know that John told me? Looking down at the men, I saw that there was little superficial difference between them, aside from coloring. They were equally tall, equally authoritative in manner, equally educated—the dark Arab in native robes, the tawny American in dinner suit. They must be nearly the same age. I thought suddenly that I should have sensed that Ibrahim was more than a servant by John's relaxed, man-to-man attitude.

John is one American with the instinctive touch for handling natives—kind, approachable, but never the least doubt about who's boss. How many evenings I'd seen him below with Ibrahim, waiting for me. Only now did I realize that, when they were alone together, John treated Ibrahim as an equal. And it was reciprocal, until the moment I appeared, when Ibrahim was at once the respectful servant.

There was one tiny but vital difference between the men. John was my husband.

5

Sheila Haysrath came to see me the next afternoon, angular and discontented as always, in a
badly fitted linen suit. I wondered at her reason;
Sheila never wasted time on a woman. Ostensibly,
it was to express Sir Percival's concerned sympa-
thy over the unpleasant incident. "You were actually *there?*" she inquired in a couldn't-care-less
voice.

"Yes, I was there." Did she wish I'd failed to
survive, leaving John legally free? "It was really
nothing," I assured her. "I expect you've seen
much worse in your time."

Surprisingly, she agreed. "Not but what it's always nervous-making if one's husband is in the
middle of a fracas. There was a horrid affair in
Kuala Lumpur years ago, everyone barricaded in
the houses, and it was twenty-four hours before I
knew Ian was cozily in Singapore all the time."
Was she inferring I was insufficiently concerned
for John's life? What in hell *was* she after?

"Oh, I'll admit to a fit of shakes when John got

home," I told her tranquilly, "but my great-great-grandma was a pioneer, and if she could stand up to Indians with tomahawks, I figure I can take whatever comes." I could tell by her expression that it wasn't the answer she wanted, that there was still something on her mind. "How are the children?" I changed the subject smoothly. Sheila never mentioned Enid or Georgie unless you asked her.

"Enid has a heat rash," she said absently. "Poor little beast, she ought to be out of this impossible climate."

I thought of the Haysrath children—two silent, scared little mice who shrank together in dumb terror when addressed, as though more accustomed to cuffs than kindness. I never went to Berthe Drouet's that I didn't see them playing in her garden, although she refused to be drawn into critical comment. "Why not? They live next door," she said indolently, "and our garden is larger than theirs. They are too small to be a trouble. *Eh, mes choux,* you are no trouble at all, are you? And already Enid 'elps Henri—her little fingers are so quick, so neat, at placing the stamps."

Now the germ of an idea came to me. With true female mulishness I wouldn't leave Qeman to sit on a beach in comfort while John faced hostile natives—but I had no doubt his mind would be easier if I weren't here. I wouldn't back down, but . . . "How much does it cost to go to Lebanon?" I asked Sheila.

"God knows. Why ask me? I've never been

there. Vacations don't exist in *our* budget, aside
from a native hotel for Ian to sleep it off."

"Would it be a good climate for Enid?"

"Probably. Anything would be better than Qeman."

"Could Ian afford to help?" I asked slowly.
"I'm not being impertinent, but John wants me to
go away, and—if you won't be offended, I'd ask
you to go as my guest. I've a little money of my
own, enough for passage money, I think."

She stared at me, suspiciously. "The children
too?"

"Particularly the children." I was on the verge
of confiding the real story, that I'd refused to go,
but the children would enable me to retreat gracefully.

Sheila said, "Are you fond of children?"

I was still thinking this was the perfect face-
saver. "Not *in toto*," I said absently, "but you said
Enid needed a change, and I thought—"

She gave me no chance to explain. "You
thought Ian would like your thinking of his children? I suppose he's said plenty about what a bad
mother I am during these cosy tea parties you've
been having."

"I'm afraid he never mentions you," I returned
coolly, repelled by her sharp eyes. Why had I
ever thought of inviting this woman? I didn't like
her, and she didn't like me. "Mostly Ian talks
about India, if you want to know."

Sheila laughed harshly. "Oh, I don't. I already

know how Ian talks. It sounds wonderful—but don't forget he's married."

"It might be easier all around if you remembered that you're married, too."

"What d'you mean by that?" she demanded, narrowing her eyes.

"I mean that if you entertain other men, you can hardly expect Ian to wear a tag marked 'Taken,' " I told her bluntly.

Sheila stood up with the speed of a striking cobra, and for a minute I half-thought she meant to slap me. But she drew back, glaring at me. "He's got a tag, all right," she said furiously. "He knows it, if you don't. All this sweet reforming influence, tea and lemonade—hah! It's been tried before, and it won't get you anywhere, either."

She'd flounced across the patio and through the lounge to the front hall before I could say as much as "Ta-ta; so long." Sitting up on my sun chair to stare after her, I could see a white-robed figure reaching the front door in two immense strides, and I thought, *If Ibrahim hadn't been there, she'd have slammed it.* I sank back against the cushions, so lost in thought that I was scarcely aware of anything—until my hand reached automatically for the iced-tea glass and found it freshly filled to the brim. "Ibrahim?"

"Yes, Mrs. Kennett?"

"Oh—thank you."

"It is nothing, madam." But he did not go away. While I was pondering Sheila's reaction (She had neither accepted nor declined my invitation—why

not? Did she not wish to go away from John?)
Ibrahim was puttering about. The ashtrays were
quietly cleaned, Sheila's glass set aside, cushions
softly plumped, a lighter silently extended for my
cigarette. It was like a French waiter in a very
good restaurant, waiting for his tip. I abandoned
thoughts of Sheila; whatever she'd come for, I felt
certain her script hadn't gone as planned. "What
is it, Ibrahim?"

He moved forward, looking faintly as if I had
caught him off base. "I have eyes all over my
head," I murmured. "What is it you want to tell
me? I'm with you now." I looked up at him and
wondered suddenly if he'd attended the Harvard-
Yale football game in Arab robes or worn Western
clothes during college. . . .

"Fatuoma is uncertain what to do with the
white evening gown, Mrs. Kennett. She has
cleaned it, so that it is fresh as new; she thinks
perhaps you will not wish to see it again, but it
seems a pity to her, for the dress was beautiful
and very becoming."

"Likewise damned expensive," I muttered, half
to myself.

"Unquestionably." Ibrahim nodded. "But worth
its cost. Fatuoma knows this also. What she does
not know is whether you will care to wear it again.
She has suggested it might be dyed a different
color, and in the meanwhile she has hung it in her
closet so that you will not be disturbed by coming
upon it unexpectedly. She asked me to speak to

you of this, Mrs. Kennett; she feared she could not explain to you properly in her limited English."

He went away with the ashes and crumpled tea napkins while I considered the white evening dress. I'd never questioned what became of it after that hideous evening. It was the measure of Fatuoma that she had not simply appropriated it and sold it for a high price in the bazaar. If I'd ever asked for it, I'd have been told it had not survived cleaning. Instead, she wanted me to know the dress was available again.

Did I want it? Would I ever be able to put it on without remembering those filthy, vicious smears that were Ross Elvig's lifeblood? Involuntarily, I winced—and involuntarily my spine stiffened and my lips tightened. Somehow his death was part of the problems in Qeman. He'd wanted to help my husband, even knowing he wasn't really welcome in our home. I decided I'd be damned for a chicken if I didn't wear that dress. Let it remind everyone of the night I'd worn it first. . . .

When Ibrahim returned, I said, "Tell Fatuoma to hang the dress in my closet—but I will tell her when I wish to wear it."

I sensed him glancing at me sharply as I finished my tea and set the glass aside. It was time to go upstairs and dress. I had a fanciful certainty that Ibrahim had initially been startled but had now followed my thought process to conclusion— also that he didn't wholly approve. But he said only, "Certainly, Mrs. Kennett. I will convey your instructions."

The telephone caught me as I reached the lower hall . . . but somehow I was unsurprised to find the white evening gown already hanging at the rear of my closet when I finally reached the bedroom. Vaguely, I wondered what had become of the white spangled evening purse I'd carried that evening. I couldn't remember if it had been stained, but it didn't matter. I had several other bags that could be used. I forgot the whole thing when John came in with his evening tie, as usual. . . .

I might never have sent the cablegram but for the scene that evening in the darkened patio of the Argentine Consulate. One of the Mexican attachés harbored a delusion that I was a breath of the frug, and after twenty minutes of jerking about like an animated Picasso, I was quite deliberately hiding in a garden chair, when I heard voices. Involuntarily, I looked around, exactly as the moon emerged from behind a cloud.

In the corner by the jasmine bushes were Sheila Haysrath and John. Sheila was crying quietly. I had to admit it was a graceful performance, but when John suddenly put his arms about her, I stuffed my chiffon handkerchief into my mouth to keep from protesting. I sat very still, unable to avert my eyes, but I was both puzzled and analytical—because it wasn't a sexy embrace. John was certainly cuddling her, soothing her, wiping her eyes with his handkerchief, murmuring softly, and laying his cheek against her hair—but from experience, I knew he could do a lot better than that.

He released her hastily at a slight noise in the darkness behind me, and they turned back to the dance floor. The moon had gone behind another cloud, but I couldn't miss his voice, "It won't be long, Sheila—I'm sure of that. And I'm always here; you know you can count on me."

Nor could I miss her silky response. "Oh, John darling, I couldn't bear it if I didn't know that. You're all I have to turn to. . . ."

When they had gone, I exhaled sharply. I think until that very moment, I'd not quite *believed* in a serious situation. I had told myself, "Wait and see," but in the press of everything else boiling up, I had half-forgotten the personal angle. Even now, with my legs feeling like second-day spaghetti, it seemed incredible. Yet how else could I interpret "It won't be long now"?

" 'Ave a cigarette?" a voice purred beside me. It was madame Drouet, ensconced like a small black sibyl in the chair to my left. I had no doubt she'd been there all the time. She leaned forward, extending a gold case. "Try one of these." Automatically, I took one. We smoked silently for a minute; then she asked casually, "*Alors,* what do you do about this?"

"I don't know," I said honestly. "It doesn't seem real."

"These things 'appen when a man is alone too long," she observed. "And they stop. I am an old woman, *chérie,* and your John is a good man.

Even good men 'ave their moments, but with a good man, the moment becomes a memory." She exhaled a long cloud of cigarette smoke. "You will do nothing."

"I'm not so sure of that," I returned slowly. "You see, I'm angry. Not at John—and I don't think there's anything for me to be angry with him about, as yet. But I have an odd feeling about Sheila Haysrath."

"Ah?"

"Yes," I went on deliberately. "I don't believe in her unhappiness with Ian. I don't think she's trapped and tied to a drunken beast. I don't know why she tries to hook every man in sight—but I don't think she'd ever leave Ian under any circumstances."

There was a long pause. "*Enfin*," madame Drouet murmured. "You are a very very clever young woman, *ma chère* Françoise."

"You agree with me?"

"Me, I am an old woman," she said again. "I 'ave been everywhere, almost. I 'ave seen many things, met many people—but they are all the same when one is my age, and I do not tell what I 'ave seen. But to you, because you are clever, I will tell something." Lazily, she drew out another cigarette, lit it from the burning butt, and crushed out the tiny end.

"Sheila Haysrath was in Teheran five years ago. *Moi, aussi*," she stated briskly. "There was a man. For Sheila there is always a man, although she does not always 'ave such *bonne chance* as to find one like John Kennett. There were the tales of unhappiness, the pitiful bruises, the drunkenness in public, the dirty house—'ow you say it? The whole bit—only the children were younger." For once I didn't laugh at her adored American slang.

"But that time there was also a woman, the wife of an Argentine attaché, and very wealthy. While Sheila is accepting the attentions of the man she has found, Mr. 'Aysrath is finding the other woman *amusante*. He calls upon her regularly for tea—*pour quelque chose*." Her voice was a shrug. "And *pouf!* There is a scene in the bazaar, a slapped face, loud voices—and shortly a transfer to Afghanistan. Now there is Qeman . . . and John Kennett."

I stood up on a deep breath, shaking my skirts into place. "I see. *Merci infiniment,* madame."

She cleared her throat delicately. "I am a nosybody," she admitted, charmingly, "but I like to know things *first*. So, please—what is her name?"

"Anita Janus," I said, and went to ask for the telephone.

Nita's cable arrived next day. Like Nita herself, it was lavish—but Nita had more money than her auditors could count, plus a vocabulary enriched by four years at Vassar with me.

ENCHANTED WITH YOUR WONDERFUL INVITATION DARLING WILL FLY OVER FROM CAIRO NEXT WEEK STOP HOPE YOU HAVE LOTS OF LUSCIOUS

MEN AVAILABLE SWEETIE STOP ABSO-
LUTELY NOTHING EXCITING IN CY-
PRUS AND GREEK ARCHIPELAGO UT-
TERLY DEADLY STOP SAVE A CUTE
LITTLE SHEIKH FOR ME PLEASE DEAR-
EST LOVE TO JOHN EVER YOURS DE-
VOTEDLY NITA

At dinnertime (for once we were eating *á deux*
in the garden) I said brightly, "Guess what, darling. Nita's coming to stay with us next week."

John's face lit up momentarily, then went worried. "I don't know, hon—with things as they are, I
hate to be responsible for an heiress. Couldn't you
meet her somewhere instead?"

I pretended to consider the point. "I can't reach
her," I fibbed. "She's on a yacht somewhere in the
Aegean, I think. Oh, let her come here, and if you
think it's dangerous, we can hop a plane the next
minute for Lebanon or whatever."

"All right. It'll probably be safe enough, at that.
Colonel Penniston's coming down from Djurdel
tomorrow."

"Who's he?"

"Fellow I knew in bomber training," John said
evasively. "Knows the Middle East like a book.
Useful chap."

I wasn't so sure. It was no part of my plan to
have a useful chap gumming the works, and ever
since freshman year, I'd known that mice and men
might make plans, but if they revolved about Anita Janus, they could go awfully haywire. Nothing

could be done about it, of course; the man was coming, presumably to ease the pressure on John in some way. I couldn't help but be glad of that. I assigned him the farthest guest room and hoped that perhaps he'd leave before Nita arrived. I was getting sick of playing everything by ear, but I had no choice, for I could think of no sensible fiction for telling him to butt out if he got in the way.

Bob Penniston was reassuringly uninteresting, although after a single glance I told myself *this* was what an FBI man would look like. He was the epitome of the man next door, the sort you wouldn't remember even if you were married to him—facially, that is. Mentally, he was another dish, though it was several days before he got around to me. Meanwhile, he was simply "John's old buddy" come for a visit. I couldn't be sure if they'd ever actually met before in their lives, but certainly they got along together most convincingly. There was no doubt in my mind that Bob was in Qeman for some official reason, but whether it was to catch the spy or connected with Ross Elvig's murder was unclear to me. Needless to say I played it straight and asked no awkward questions. I'm afraid I felt a bit superior: *Let the little boys play games and think they're fooling me.*

Out of respect for Ramadan, the foreign colony gave only informal parties, into which Bob fitted with ease. I noticed he seemed on good terms with

Sheila, but she was still concentrating on John. Madame Drouet eyed me with a basilisk gaze but said nothing. For my part, I managed to be looking the other way whenever Sheila got John outside—which was every evening and lasted *interminably*. I would *not* let myself speculate on how matters were progressing, in spite of a growing suspicion that perhaps Bob was there only to keep me from noticing. . . . If he was intended purely as a red herring, he did his job well—dancing with me frequently but not making it a rush. I insisted to myself that I'd figured out the true state of affairs and had no cause to be anguished—but the fact remained that there was a subtle difference.

For one thing, Ian was away—and for another, Sheila's behavior was verging on the brazen. It was as though she didn't give a damn, as though *now* was the moment and she meant to have everything settled before Ian returned. Most disheartening of all, John not only permitted her barefaced appropriation, right under my nose, but was looking fatuous. He was kind and courteous when we were together, which wasn't often because of Bob, but the *coup de grâce* was my realization that he'd been sleeping in his own room ever since Bob arrived. It was supposed to be for fear of disturbing me, while the boys enjoyed bull sessions of auld lang syne. Heaven knows what they talked about or when they came upstairs, but it was far more disturbing to awaken alone in one half of a double bed.

I grinned and bore it, pinning my faith to Nita's

arrival, although if Ian didn't come back, my plan would be useless. I was practically counting the minutes and in no mood for intrigue when Bob joined me for late breakfast one morning. After half an hour of thrust and parry, he gave up the casual approach and said, "John was right we'd better tell you, but the bigwigs insisted it'd be wiser if not even my hostess knew my real mission."

"Mission?" I echoed innocently.

He looked at me sharply out of ordinary hazel eyes and snorted. "Telephone John?" he suggested politely.

I surprised him—I did phone John. When I got back to the table, I said, "All right; what d'you want to know?"

"Everything," he said tersely, hauling out a small black notebook. "Who's sleeping with whom, what sort of toothpaste they use, every word you've overheard and everything you suspect. Start with the servants and proceed to the foreign colony—and don't let's waste time on loyalty or friendships, shall we?"

Well, I omitted one thing—Sheila Haysrath's possible affair with my husband. But as far as I was concerned she was only A Thing. Whatever the reality, Bob either already knew it, or it had nothing to do with the case. When I'd finished, he merely said, "Hmmmm, thanks."

I wondered what he thought, but Nita's plane was due shortly, so I said only, "Hope it helps— we'll meet at dinner."

＊　＊　＊

I stood at the airport, where so few months previously John had met me and Ross Elvig had entered our lives. I wondered sadly if it might have been better had I never come. Would Ross have evaded his killer if he hadn't meant to tell me something? Did it make any difference that John's wife was here, to see for herself his preoccupation with Sheila?

In my eagerness for Nita, I was nearly an hour early. I stood at the barrier; I walked into the lounge and had a Coke from the machine that's the ubiquitous symbol of capitalist supremacy. As usual, the planes were arriving one after another. Sipping the drink, I wandered back to the arrival gate, hearing the fuzzy intercom announcing, "Four four one from Paris. . . . Two oh three from Athens. . . . One two five from Calcutta. . . ." I was listening for 651 from Capetown-Nairobi-Cairo, but idly watching the great planes circling and landing smoothly one after another, so close together that I was lost in admiration at the skill of the pilots and landing-tower instructions. I'd always wanted to learn how to fly, so I could understand John when he talked about planes. He had the sort of license that's good for anything anywhere in the world, apparently, except scheduled flights—and that's only a union technicality. The number of hours I'd sat alone staring at the Indian Ocean or assorted mountains, while John was fraternizing with the lads up front!

But every time I had wanted to take lessons,
John had always interviewed the instructor first—
and come back looking *tall*; so I'd practically
given up the whole idea. I wondered now whether
he'd approve anyone here. It was unquestionably
the biggest, most efficient airport we'd hit, being
almost literally on the crossroads of the world. Qeman (in Arabic, the Q is pronounced like a hard
G, so that Qatar sounds like GUT'r, Qeman is
g'MAN) is the refueling point for airlines between
Europe and India, as well as between Africa and
eastern Europe. In general, local Middle East
traffic occurs in the morning: Riyadh to Mecca,
Aden to Basta, Alexandria to Teheran and Baku.
The en route long distance flights arrive in the
afternoon.

Restlessly, I wandered along the wire barrier
away from the arrivals and transferees, to the far
end, where I could see the smaller runways. A private desert plane was landing, and soon a digni-
fied procession of white-robed figures descended
the steps. They lined up, forming a corridor, while
a typical short, bearded man appeared, obviously
a local tribal chief. Judging by the honor-guard
formation, he was very powerful. He stood on the
top platform, gathering his robes into one hand,
while a second man emerged from the plane. He
was taller, but equally hirsute and robed, leaning
to the other's ear with some remark that drew a
broad laugh. The sun glinted brightly from several
gold teeth, before the bigshot set his hand on the
railing and descended, with the other Arabs unob-

trusively lending a firm hand to the older man's elbow. Number One Son, I decided, and was about to turn away, when something made me take another glance.

The whole group was disappearing swiftly toward a clutch of limousines. The sheikh and his son (if it was his son) led the way; the honor guard bringing up the rear obscured the two figures, so it wasn't easy to see. Still, I'd have sworn the tall man wasn't an Arab. His stride was— different. Almost I'd have thought it was John— except he was in Qeman and hadn't a beard. But there was something familiar about that figure. I craned forward for a better look, and behind me the fuzzy intercom announced, "Flight six five one now arriving from Cairo . . ."

6

I forgot everything, ditched the empty Coke bottle in a trash basket, and raced for the arrival gate, politely elbowing my way to the very front of the barrier, through which I stuck my nose. After a while a great silvery monster swooped out of the blue and deposited Anita Janus at my feet. Metaphorically, of course. Never had any pilot taken so long to taxi about and adjust his tail satisfactorily. Never had airport help taken so long to place the landing steps. But eventually they got the airplane door open, and there she was—incredibly beautiful, as always.

Long and intimately as I'd known her, I never got over each first sight of Nita. Her beauty was authentic, chiseled. It owed nothing whatever to her *couturier* (whoever she was patronizing this season). I'd seen her at five in the morning after a strenuous Princeton prom; I'd seen her in dungarees digging clams in Maine; I'd seen her with a hangover; and I'd seen her when she'd just lost the man she loved in Vietnam. No matter what happened to her, she was always beautiful. Phidias would have gone out of his mind if he'd ever seen her, and Leonardo da Vinci would never have bothered with the Gioconda.

And she had two million dollars, all for herself.

She stood on the top landing step, ignoring the men eagerly attempting to assist her downward, and glanced along the line of people waiting at the barrier, until her eyes picked me out. With a wave of her hand and a brilliant smile, she allowed herself to be tenderly led down to the tarmac, where she kindly but firmly dismissed the cavaliers. I didn't have to hear; I could have done the script from the top after nearly ten years.

Finally, she rushed forward and kissed me with abandon. "Fran, you look wonderful, but wonderful!"

"So do you," I returned, my spirits rising. With Nita in Qeman, I had the most powerful ally—beauty, brains, and money. Between the two of us, if we couldn't put "paid" to Sheila Haysrath, we didn't deserve our Vassar diplomas.

She was a total joy in other ways, because hers was a "noticing" personality. When we went in for customs inspection, we were respectfully whisked from the general line—to face the man who remembered *my* name. He opened her luggage, pretended to glance inside, reclosed it, and bowed us forward to the VIP exit, expressing a hope that Mrs. Kennett's guest would enjoy Qeman.

Nita noticed. "Well, well," she remarked, as we paraded grandly forth to the car. "I only own most of that airline—but I can see I am as dirt, merely tolerated because I am visiting Mrs. Kennett. How lovely for you to be a personage, darling."

I chuckled, but I knew she meant it. All her money had never made Nita bored or blasé, or anything but genuine and affectionate with those she loved. I wasn't her only intimate—I knew that—but with no family of her own ("not so much as a fourth cousin twice removed"), Nita had unconsciously looked for substitute relatives, wanting nothing but to be part of a *home*. Once she'd said, "It's no fun being an orphan, but if you're rich, you don't even get foster parents. And a house may not be a home, but neither is a bank. The only possible good is being able to choose a family; at least you end up with people you like."

By the time we met—two dumb freshmen in Poughkeepsie, New York—she had a "brother" and a couple of "aunts" and "cousins." She picked me to be "sister" after two weeks of college, when mother's weekly letter said, "love to Nita." She spent every vacation in Toledo with me, as a matter of course, and upset all airline schedules pulling rank to get home from Tokyo for Daddy's funeral.

All the way from the airport, now, she leaned from the car, exclaiming, pointing out things, asking questions. Insensibly I regained my original pleasure in Qeman when I saw it anew through Nita's eyes. The crowning touch was her delight in my home. "This is it? Well, you *are* coming up in the world, darling. When I think of some of the horrors you've inhabited, with pythons in the attic . . ."

I giggled, but it was true, though I'd never dared tell mother. In Timor, we had had a python overhead, and we had loved him dearly. He had been too big to get into our part of the house, but he had eaten the rats—which could get in.

After Larry's death in Vietnam, Nita traveled a lot. Wherever I went with John, she always came "to see for myself"—and spent a week in Toledo as soon as she got home, telling mother all about it. By the time she arrived in Timor, we'd named the python Oliver (which John considers a long, slithery name) and were so used to his nocturnal rustlings that we scarcely heard them. I have always suspected she wangled John's immediate transfer, although she professes to own no Madison Mines stock. All the same, that particular transfer was too fortuitous to be completely on John's merit, considerable as this may have been—and *she* never told mother about Oliver Python either.

"I am the victim of sudation, totally dehydrated, parched, and desiccated," she announced, crawling out of the car. "In other words, I am dying of thirst, but the instant we've had something cold and wet, I demand a conducted tour of this establishment."

"You ain't seen nothin' yet," I assured her, glimpsing Ibrahim materializing like a jinn as usual, to open the front door. I never knew how he did it, but it is a fact that although the hall might seem to be empty, and there was a doorbell,

no visitor—however unexpected—ever had to ring.
I couldn't resist saying, grandly, "Oh, Nita, this is
Ibrahim, my steward. Ibrahim, please have the
luggage taken to Miss Janus's room and send iced
tea to the patio."

I should have known better, of course. She murmured, "How do you do, Ibrahim," and made
great amused eyes at me while he bowed.

"Good afternoon, Miss Janus. The staff is happy
to welcome Mrs. Kennett's friend. We hope you
will enjoy your visit." Ibrahim turned to me. "I
have taken the liberty of engaging Fatuoma's sister, Zoe, to serve Miss Janus, since she is traveling
without a maid. I trust that will meet with your
approval, madam? She is less experienced, but her
English is better, and with Fatuoma's guidance,
we may hope she will be satisfactory to Miss
Janus."

I restrained myself from saying, "How do *you*
know she's traveling without a maid?" Nita suddenly became regal. "I'm certain Zoe will be ade-
quate," she said indifferently, "or you would not
have employed her."

"Thank you, Miss Janus. This way, if you
please. I regret I was unable to procure any Pall
Malls today; there were only Mrs. Kennett's usual
brand and some filter-tipped varieties. But the
shop has promised to obtain yours by tomorrow."

Well! I murmured, "Thank you, Ibrahim," and
mentally kicked myself. John had obviously told
him he'd told *me*, and Ibrahim was daring to have
a bit of private fun in return for that "steward"

bit. I could have appreciated it—except that I knew Nita. She sank into the chair he assured her was comfortable and looked at me dazedly.

When he had departed, she asked, "Who *dat?*"

There was no point in covering up. "He's an umpty-eighth cousin of the Sheikh."

"Oh? Why have they planted the local FBI man in your house, sweetie? Are you smuggling something?"

"Naturally. John has the bhang concession."

"Then why that bed of poppies?" She looked across the garden.

"I do a bit of opium on the side."

"Oh, *good!*" she said cordially. "It's always wise to be diversified—or so my brokers tell me." And she plunged into a description of the Greek islands until Ibrahim had come and gone, leaving the iced tea behind. "Now," she said briskly, "what's wrong, Fran?"

"Oh, dear, does it show that plainly?"

"Not to the casual eye, but you can't fool me, darling. I deduce someone's making eyes at John." She lit a cigarette thoughtfully. "You wouldn't send for me if it concerned business—unless it was monkey business. Begin at the beginning, please."

"You witch! She's an English girl, married to an attaché, and she makes a specialty of appealing to male chivalry. To hear her talk, her husband is a drunken devil who beats her to a pulp every night of the week, but she hasn't enough money to leave him, and no place to go."

"So?"

"So I don't believe a word of it," I said, flatly. "I'm convinced she wouldn't let Ian go to the corner without her. She's got two kids, poor little tykes, but when I invited her to bring them to Lebanon if Ian would pay half, she pounced on it as trying to impress *him*."

"Where do I come in? Don't tell me you couldn't handle this yourself, Fran, after that consul's daughter, and the widow in Lourenço Marques . . . or are you afraid of upsetting John?"

"Partly," I admitted. "This time is different, Nita. It got under way while I was home. And John didn't really want me to join him—I realize that now. Anyway, he hardly noticed the others, but he *sees* Sheila—if you know what I mean? I can tell everybody thinks there's something to it, even Ian; but what I can't tell is whether Ian would like to be rid of her, or how deeply John's emotions are involved.

"Ian's underfoot at teatime nearly every day, unless he's off on assignment to the desert. I don't much like him, Nita, but he's fantastically handsome, and he knows how to make a good story out of the posts he's had. John hasn't said anything; he's never here at teatime—if he's anywhere, he's with Sheila while Ian's sitting it out here. . . ."

"Cox and Box?"

"Perhaps—and there's a chance my being friendly with Ian would seem a perfect solution, but the real reason I sent for you is that you're rich."

"Well! That's a bald statement."

"Yes, but it's the crux of the matter. Look—I'm certain she'll never let Ian go, not even for John, who's a much better bet financially. I don't think Ian could ever appear sufficiently interested in me to upset Sheila, because she knows I'm not wealthy. But from information received, I understand that's the one way to open it up. If he falls for a rich woman, she'll blow her stack."

Nita considered the outline for a moment. "You want me to fascinate a lush with my wealth and beauty, in the hope that his wife will think I'm taking him seriously," she translated, "leading to a chain reaction of jealousy that will disillusion John?"

"More or less, and it may not work," I said painfully. "There's a first time for everything, and if she's really got John in her pocket, she might figure to switch from one bill-payer to another. But another thing I don't believe is that Ian has to drink or is ever as drunk as he seems. I don't believe any of it, Nita, but at the risk of making John unhappy to find she's merely played with his affections, I want to drag it into the light. Right now, before it goes any further." I looked at Nita squarely. "You're family; you've gathered John's here for an oil contract."

She nodded. "It figured."

"It's a short-term assignment, ends when the contract is signed. Then he'll be sent . . . somewhere. So you see? It's only a month or six weeks. If we can break it up, it'll be easier on John—he'll be leaving anyway, and he'll have a new assignment to absorb any sorrows. I'm staking everything I've got—which is John—on your being a catalyst," I finished. "I can't do it alone this time, even if I could get through to him. Even if I could manage the rumpus, he'd only be disillusioned with me, too. Are you with me?"

"To the death," she said instantly. "Not that I think there's the least danger of your losing John. You've always underestimated your magnetic potential, Fran. Still, if it's being noticed, it had better be nipped before it leaves a mark on his dossier. Facts, please—who are these people, what strategy do I use, do I come on strong or wait to be wooed, do I display intelligence or flutter, et cetera. Refill the iced-tea glasses and start the briefing—or," she asked suddenly, "is this place bugged?"

"I doubt it. I wouldn't dispute a possible ear to the door, but a mike would be the first thing John and Baker would look for."

She raised her eyebrows. "That serious?" At my nod, she said, "Hmmmm. Well, well! Commies?"

"Nobody knows, but John thinks not; he says it doesn't fit."

"Nationalists, then. Sometimes I think we should never have told anyone about the American Revolution," she remarked. "It seems to give the most half-baked inspirations to other people, not but what the guillotine complete with tum-

brels and madame Defarge, would be better than
what the Russians got. Well, begin the précis."

I talked for a solid hour, spurred on by her inci-
sive questions. We were interrupted once, when
Fouad brought a fresh bucket of ice and another
pitcher of tea, under the supervision of Ibrahim.
Nita switched instantly to admiration of the
shrubbery, and added casually, "*Qui est ce type-
lá, qui a besoin d'un bain?*"

I happened to be glancing at Ibrahim, and I distinctly saw his lips twitch. "*C'est notre garçon,*" I
told her repressively. "Go on about Athens; it
sounds fascinating." As soon as the servants had
retired, I said, "It's no good using French; Ibrahim's a Harvard man."

Nita choked on her tea. "Good God!"

"Hasty Pudding, and *summa cum laude.* I don't
know whether he understands Italian and Ger-
man, but he got your comment on Fouad."

"Then perhaps he'll see to it the man *takes* a
bath," Nita returned vigorously. "All right; back
to the main stream. . . ." When I'd finished, she
murmured, "Mmm. Okay; when do we go to
work?"

"Tonight, if Ian's back in Qeman." Something
stirred in my subconscious, but I couldn't identify
it. I let it go and stood up. "Come on; I'll show
you around before the boys get back."

"Boys?"

"John and a suppositious pal of his named Penniston. I think he's really Interpol or something,

but he's quite nice," I muttered in her ear. That question about "bugging" was making me extra-cautious, although I didn't believe in anything more than native grapevine. I forgot the whole thing while I took her about the house. Our conversation as we went from room to room was entirely woman-talk. Nita opened every door and every drawer (literally) and made frank comments.

Ibrahim was accompanying us, I realized. Very unobtrusively, but surfacing every now and then to open a door or warn Miss Janus of an unexpected step. By the time we'd made the tour and reached her room, Nita was being regal again. "It's basically a perfect house, except for those pink tiles in the service pantry," she said languidly, without looking behind her. "Don't you agree, Ibrahim?"

"Yes and no," he murmured impersonally. "In general, a visitor would never see them, Miss Janus."

"I suppose not, but I am part cat, and you know how cats can never be comfortable until they've explored every corner."

"Mohammed tells us no house can be a home until a cat chooses to live in it," he returned, and backed away, bowing politely. "I will send Zoe to you, Miss Janus."

For the first time I wondered if Ibrahim was married, because if my Harvard-educated relative of the Sheikh could so far forget himself as to make that sort of subtle compliment . . . Nita closed the door and snorted. "If you could see your expression, Fran! I'm wondering if he's married too."

"Oh, dear—he's never before . . . I mean . . ."

She laughed heartily. "Use your head, sweetie! If he's local Intelligence, he's got a complete run-down on me, even to the brand of cigarettes I pre-fer—so he also knows perfectly well you've told me All. On the whole, I think it's a compliment to both of us—that he dares unbend a bit."

"Perhaps. I still wonder if he's married."

"Oh, undoubtedly. Probably only one wife, if he's Western educated—although I've known a number of Harvard men who were enthusiastic about polygamy."

We were in the lounge—John, Bob, and myself—when Nita came floating down the stairs in a cas-ual little flame chiffon rag that cost the earth and did startling things for her creamy skin and raven's-wing hair. Bob saw her first and choked on his drink, which is the normal reaction of all males anywhere on initial sight of Nita. John was the same way at first, but through the years he has grown used to her. He was able, now, to greet her warmly but calmly as she said, "How's my fa-vorite brother-in-law?"

While they were hugging each other, Bob sud-denly came out of his trance "This is your *sister?*" he asked, with unflattering disbelief.

"Adopted," I told him soothingly. "Nita, this is Colonel Bob Penniston, who's an old friend of

John's. Drink fast, kiddies, or we'll be rudely late."

The social chore for the evening was a dinner dance wingding at the Russian Embassy, completely black tie. The Russians paid no attention to Ramadan. Why should they consider other people's religion, when they'd none of their own? I was dying to see Nita's impact on the party line. The older generation might fail to respond (although Stalin had three wives, so apparently sex is one thing that can survive Marx), but I was privately betting that Gregor Semirov and the other boys wouldn't be proof against all that beauty wrapped in good capitalist dollars.

At the entrance we met the Haysraths with Sir Percival. Sheila's green eyes flicked over Nita with the speed and thoroughness of roentgen rays, while Ian bowed politely, and Sir Percival's face lit up. "Ah, Hrmmmm, delighted to meet ye, Miss Janus. How long ye goin' to stay? Must put on a bit of a show for her, what? Haysrath, those Bedouins of yours—they anywhere about? Might fix up a camel race, eh? Ever seen one, Miss Janus? Damnedest thing y'ever saw . . . great ugly brutes galumphin' along, natives yellin' like banshees. Placin' bets, y'know. . . ."

Sir Percival's voice bumbled away, more Old School Tie than usual, as he gallantly handed Nita forward. The rest of us followed in an untidy group. In the entrance hall I found Ian at my elbow. He looked a bit disturbed, but I was too glad to find him in Qeman to worry about his problems. Plan A could start at once. "I wish you'd take Nita under your wing," I murmured to him. "Until she knows who's who, I'd be grateful if you'd help keep off the rabble."

He stared at her creamy shoulders under the diaphanous evening cape for a moment. "I'll probably be killed in the crush, but anything to assist."

"She's quite a responsibility," I sighed. "All that *money*—two million bucks, you know. And what her family will say if I don't protect her from undesirables!"

"If she's still *Miss* Janus, with that face and money besides, I'd suppose she's well able to separate sheep from goats without surveillance," he remarked, but I sensed a reaction—as though he were pricking up his ears.

"It's more than that. John really didn't want her here, because of all the native unrest. He's got enough on his mind, and if he's got to worry about her, it'll ruin Bob's visit."

"Who is this Penniston?" Ian asked.

"Old army buddy of John's—first time they've had a chance to get together for years." I shrugged. "Which is why, thank heavens you're back, Ian. When did you get in?"

"This afternoon," he said absently, still looking at Nita, who was going away to the ladies' cloakroom with a final seductive glance for Sir Percival. "All right, Fran; I'll keep an eye on her, as well as old Perce. Not sure he won't need more protection than your friend!" He grinned.

I laughed and started up the stairs. At the landing I glanced back, to see Ian moving away from me across the entrance hall—and despite the difference in perpective, I knew why the tall man accompanying the desert sheikh at the airport had seemed familiar. Of course. It had been Ian; he'd shaved off the beard—that was all. We all knew he'd been away; Sir Percival had asked about "those Bedouins"; and they *were* around. I had seen them . . . meaning we were in for a camel race unless Ian could get us out of it—and he probably couldn't.

Sir Percival had the memory of an elephant. Having hit upon his concept of a treat for Nita, he'd keep after it with British bulldoggishness. I sighed inwardly, continuing upward. I have *been* to a camel race. It is, indeed, exciting—likewise smelly beyond description. Everybody sweats freely, complicated by the camels, who are neither housebroken nor genteel. Upon reflection I thought I'd ask Nita to speak to Ian. I'd no idea what his job really was, but I'd noticed he always became a bit official if one asked wheres and whens. He might rather I hadn't seen him—and British Embassy business was no concern of mine, after all.

He was waiting for us at the foot of the stairs when we came down. "Any friend of Fran's is a friend of all of us," he told Nita. "We hope you're going to stay a long, long time."

"How sweet of you. If everyone is like you, Mr. Haysrath, I may never go home at all."

"Study me well, and render judgment later,"

Ian murmured, drawing her into the salon. They made a breathtaking couple, I realized—both tall, slender, black-haired. Evidently, he agreed with me, beginning with fiddling the dinner seating plan. Somehow, Ian took Nita in to dinner, which was entirely against protocol. I don't think he introduced her to anyone, although a few determined souls got madame Tomyienkov to present them. Perhaps Gregor was a better Communist than I'd thought, for he devoted himself to Sheila as usual without a glance for Nita. Sir Percival made a beeline for her after dinner, and I could see her flirting with him very prettily over coffee and liqueurs, but once he'd gone off to the bridge tables, Ian took over.

He drank almost nothing that night, danced every dance he could get with Nita, and whisked her to the garden for every intermission. The very ease with which Plan A was succeeding made me oddly uncertain. Madame Drouet was looking thoughtful—her seat at the bridge table commanded a view of the doors to the garden—but when we passed each other on the stairs to the lavabo, she said only, *"Elle est charmante, votre amie.* For 'er, when I tell 'im, I think Henri will emerge."

I said, "I'd like them to meet. She's not a philatelist, but she still has her father's collection."

"Ah? Bring 'er day after tomorrow, so I 'ave time to prepare Henri for a treat," she said briskly. "You and I can gossip while they—'ow you say?— chop their teeth at each other. *A bientôt, ma chére.*" With a final wave of the hand, she was gone—leaving me to guffaw privately at the picture of Nita and old Henri jabbering together.

Toward the end of the evening, Ian's behavior seemed to penetrate Sheila's consciousness. She began peering over John's shoulder instead of into his eyes, and she was right *there* with her hand possessively tucked into the crook of Ian's elbow when we said goodnight.

The next morning Nita curled up on the chaise longue in my bedroom and said flatly, "It isn't going to work."

"Yes; I was afraid of that. Reasons?"

She took a sip of coffee, gazing absently at the wall, while Zoe and Fatuoma were darting about, creating tidiness and perfect comfort until their ladies should choose to bathe and dress for the day. I noted a package of Pall Malls placed beside Nita—so Ibrahim had already been to the bazaar. When the maids had gone, she said, "No reason— only a hunch. I think he suspects . . . something. He's intrigued enough to play, until he figures it out. We may still pull it off, depending on how well Sheila knows him. She didn't strike me as having the wits of a flea, but nobody is ever as dumb as you think 'em."

I nodded, feeling discouraged. "I thought it was looking too easy. I don't think she knows him half as well as he knows her, and after the incident in Teheran, he's likely to be extra careful. Well, all we can do is try."

"Oh, definitely. Tell me about Bob Penniston; he's rather a dear, isn't he?"

"I don't know anything to tell. He's an old army buddy of John's, but I never met him before. Do you like him?" I'd decided to say nothing of Ross Elvig and the subsequent events. They had nothing to do with Nita's visit, and I thought we'd have a better chance of success if she were completely unaware, unguarded in speech.

She looked at me sharply but said only, "Yes; I like him. He's the sort that fits anywhere. Any objection if I play him against Ian?"

"None, if you can," I returned—dubiously, because in spite of his first reaction, Bob Penniston looked to be at least forty and designed by nature to be someone's uncle. "What shall we do today? It's the Greeks tonight; resign yourself to native music. Which reminds me—for heaven's sake tell Ian to quash that camel race!"

"I already did. I've been to one too." She held her nose delicately. "Could we poke about the town?"

"Of course." I suddenly remembered the rug shop where I'd seen Ross. Between this and that, I had never investigated. Now was the time. Because of Ramadan, I felt certain we would be safe enough. After the one demonstration, Qeman had settled down and absorbed itself in its holiday ritual. There had been no more open unrest, although the sense of reserve and withdrawal persisted. "This afternoon we'll go to the bazaar," I said.

* * *

We went first to the English book shop, where I told Selim to meet us at the entrance to the native quarter in an hour. "Ah-yes'm." He grinned happily, and I could see him parking the car in readiness, disposing himself for a siesta as we entered the store. He was dozing placidly over the wheel when we'd worked our way along the street half an hour later and turned into the *souk*. I made straight for the rug shop, dragging Nita with me.

It was a typical native store, though rather large and more luxurious than most. There was a front section filled with lovely rugs of all sizes, and several cases of jewelry tucked about cunningly to catch the eye. The displays were unusually tasteful and discreet; instead of the ordinary jumble, there were single items for contemplation. At the rear, hardly visible in the shadows, a series of small rugs were used as curtains to the interior—where the owner and his family lived. A muted jabber of Arabic attested their presence, probably engaged in a *Kaffeeklatsch*.

We had come so exactly at the ending of siesta that the shop was still deserted, although the door was open and a jangly bell announced customers. Nita was already inspecting the jewelry cases, but for a full moment we were alone. Then a rear rug was pulled aside hastily, and to my astonishment, Fatuoma came forward. She was equally surprised to see me, and deeply distressed. "Madam, why you come? You need, you *send* for me."

I could sense her trembling. Poor kid; so she

wasn't supposed to be off duty, but she'd chanced running home for a minute when I'd apparently gone out for the afternoon? "No, no," I assured her, smiling. "I didn't come for you, Fatuoma. I didn't even know you lived here. We are looking at the shops, that's all."

Her English was so uncertain that I wasn't sure she understood, but fortunately Nita said, "Fatuoma, what is the price of this bracelet?" and the girl understood we hadn't come in search of her like tyrants. She stopped trembling and smiled at me shyly. "Not know, is not home, is shop of"—she frowned, trying to remember the word—"brother of father?"

"Your uncle."

"Unkel," she repeated carefully, and giggled. "I get. You wait?"

I nodded, and she retreated to the rug curtains. But by now my eyes were dark-adapted, and I could see the family group within, white-robed figures, seated in a ring about a brazier holding a long-spouted brass coffeepot. Fatuoma merely held the rugs aside, leaning in to speak rapidly, so I had a clear view of the party—and one pudgy man. He turned to appraise the girl's slender figure with an Arabic comment that was undoubtedly lewd, judging by the chorus of sly grins and chuckles.

It was the same desert sheikh Ian had been escorting at the airport. When he grinned fatly at the reception of his remark, I could see the gold teeth. It figured; Ross had said he was making arrange-

ments for a desert trip. Probably Fatuoma's uncle
was the local equivalent of American Express, although as he emerged from the rear room he
looked to be the typical oily-skinned rug dealer.
He came forward, clasping his hands in the formal
Eastern greeting and smiling ingratiatingly.

"Madame Kennett, I am Azriel ibn-Ferid, at
your service. You honor this humble shop with
your presence. All is at your command, if anything
is worthy of your notice." By his shrug, this was
implied as highly unlikely, so we were obviously
in for a session of shrewd bargaining.

"Thank you, Azriel," I said languidly, "but I
fear we have disturbed you with your friends. Perhaps we should leave and return at a more con-
venient moment for you?"

"No, no," he protested swiftly. "You will understand, these are not friends—merely my brother
brings a few companions to visit."

"Ah, that is why Fatuoma is here?"

"Yes; it is not often she has the chance to see
her family, and I have summoned her. If you are
displeased, the fault is mine. Already she is preparing to return . . ."

From the apologetic tone, I knew I was in the
catbird seat. Azriel didn't want his niece to lose
her good job; he'd be inclined toward magnanim-
ity. "Of course Fatuoma must visit with her family—but she has only to ask for the necessary time.
Tell her to wait; she can return with us." I
shrugged casually. "There is a seat beside Selim—
but now, if you please," I cut across his humble

thanks, "Miss Janus has found something that . . . *may* interest her, if the price is right." I waved him grandly forward to Nita, who took it from there, being as well versed with Eastern bargaining as I.

She did an expert job of it, deflecting him to a ring first, and eventually ending with the bracelet she wanted for a giveaway price, while I rambled about, exhibiting a complete lack of interest. The rugs *were* lovely. I debated a small hall runner for Mother but finally opted against. Moving from one to another, I was conscious that Azriel was keeping a sharp eye on my progress, and the nearer I got to the curtain rugs, the more nervous and watchful he became—until at length he concluded the bargaining in a rush and literally called me away. "See—if you please, Mrs. Kennett—approve your friend's taste."

I wondered if he'd been afraid I wouldn't know better than to intrude on the family, but I turned obediently and went back to agree that the bracelet was, indeed, well chosen. There was no doubt that Azriel was relieved, but he was still uneasy. Instantly, he was wrapping, falling all over himself with gratitude . . . and making no attempt to sell anything else. "We are honored by your purchase, our shop is yours, we look forward to welcoming you soon again. . . . I will send Fatuoma at once, it shall not happen again. . . ."

Nita eyed me expressionlessly while Azriel was bowing me toward the door. I raised an eyebrow, and she circled about him to the rear, calling over her shoulder, "Fran, what about this one for Tom—they've moved into a bigger house in Bala Cynwyd."

Perforce, Azriel stepped aside, and I went to examine the rug. We were exactly in front of the curtain rugs to the inner room, from which there was a spate of Arabic, interspersed with laughter. By the sound, the party was growing. I never knew a Levantine shopkeeper who placed *anything* before a good business deal, but there was now no doubt of Azriel's desire to be rid of us entirely. It was more than a possible ignorant trespass; he was right there to prevent, blocking the entrance—and hurriedly pricing the rug so ridiculously low as to preclude bargaining. In a way, we were neatly caught. When we hesitated, Azriel insisted he'd bring the rug to my house, where we could see it on the floor before making a decision.

Nita bought the thing at once. As she said later, "He'd have liked nothing better than *not* selling that rug in the shop. If he could have brought it to the house, he'd have said he was mistaken in the price, a thousand apologies, and so on. I don't think he twigged we were teasing, Fran, but if he was so anxious to get back to the party . . . Well, it was too good a buy to pass up, and someone will like it." At the time, she was shrewd enough to insist upon full payment and taking the rug with us. Azriel agreed to anything and everything, so we allowed him to sweep us away from that back room to the front of the shop, where the Arabic babble was only a murmur—but not before I'd heard A Voice.

It was a new visitor, warmly greeted by those already present. The interchange was rapid Arabic that drew laughter, but even while Azriel was rolling the rug, accepting payment, and trotting us firmly to the outer street, where Selim assisted in stowing the purchase in the trunk of the car, I knew that voice was familiar to me. Not Ian—his voice was higher-pitched—nor John, who is basso profundo . . . John's Arabic isn't that fluent, anyway.

Azriel had bowed himself away. I was unsurprised to find Zoe, as well as Fatuoma, standing humbly beside the car, awaiting my pleasure. "Sit beside Selim—there's room for both of you," I said absently, while Nita disposed herself in the rear. I crawled in beside her and said, "Home, Selim." But I was still puzzled by the familiarity of that voice.

Nita lit a cigarette quietly and stared from the window, while I pondered. Where had I heard it? It had to be someone I knew quite well, or I wouldn't have recognized the timbre when the words were incomprehensible. Coupled with Azriel's anxiety when we lingered in his shop, there was obviously more than merely wanting to get back to the party. I concentrated on all the voices I might know, closing my eyes and trying to remember.

In the end, I came up with Ibrahim, Gregor Se-

mirov, and Henri Drouet. As we drew up before
the house and I saw that Ibrahim was already visible at the front door, I was wondering frivolously
if "Henri 'ad emerged." Yet the thought was not
so frivolous after all, when I recalled his rapier-
sharp glance the night Ross Elvig was killed. . . .

7

"Something more than meets the eye?" Nita asked, over her glass of iced tea in the shaded patio.

"Yes, but I don't know what."

"Don't fuddle your mind, sweetie; it'll come to you. Where do we go tonight?"

"The Greeks'. Informal—although with madame Iandouros, the only way you can tell is if the skirt is short or long, and as John says, who's looking at hemlines?"

"She was the middle-aged Tanagra with overtones of Bali?"

"That's the one."

"Well, as between tiny feet and large breasts, I suppose she's picked the right emphasis," Nita observed indolently. "Few men look that far below the belt, after all. I think I'll finish my tea upstairs in the bathtub, Fran, and write a couple of letters."

"Suit yourself," I told her agreeably. But she didn't, after all. Ibrahim was coming out just as we stood up. "Yes, Ibrahim?"

"Mr. Haysrath asks if Miss Janus will receive him, madam."

"Of course," she said promptly, sitting down again without looking at me.

"D'you mind if I don't join you, Nita? I think I'll finish my tea upstairs and write a few letters. Show Mr. Haysrath out here, please, Ibrahim—and I expect we'll need more ice."

"Very good, madam."

I lingered just long enough to welcome Ian and to say, "Will you excuse me? I *must* write home."

"How tactful you are, dear one," Ian murmured, bending over Nita's hand. I was right—his was not the hauntingly familiar tone I'd heard in Azriel's shop.

I grinned at him. "Aren't I? See you later, laddie." I had gone across the lounge and was starting upstairs, when Ibrahim came after me. "Madam, may I have a word?"

"Of course, Ibrahim." I paused on the third step, which brought my eyes on a level with his (*His* wasn't the voice, either, I thought, even though in order to be at my front door, he'd have needed the wings of an angel; I wouldn't have put them past Ibrahim.)

"You and Miss Janus visited a rug shop today," he stated. "Please do not go again to Azriel's, Mrs. Kennett."

"Why?" I asked after a moment.

"It is not a suitable place for two ladies alone."

"Surely Fatuoma's relatives are trustworthy? I had a distinct impression Azriel was awfully anxious I shouldn't dismiss her for being there without permission."

"If you please, do not go again," he repeated stubbornly. I suppose my expression must have been equally stubborn, because he went on, "I should not like to be forced to tell Mr. Kennett, madam."

"That sounds uncommonly like a threat to 'tell teacher,' Ibrahim—and Mr. Kennett will want to know why too," I said coolly. "What's more, as soon as you've told him, I'll get it out of him, and well you know it—so you may as well tell me at once."

He nodded soberly. "You and Miss Janus are far too young and beautiful to visit any of the shops in the *souk* unescorted—particularly at this moment, Mrs. Kennett, when Qeman is filled with desert people in a holiday mood. You are right that Fatuoma's local relatives will respect you, but tribesmen can be wild and lawless. They are inclined to act first and think later—they know it is nearly impossible to exercise the Sheikh's justice in the desert. Please, Mrs. Kennett," he said earnestly, "do not tempt fate."

"Very well, Ibrahim. I promise we won't go to the *souk* alone again until Ramadan is ended and you tell me it's safe," I told him. "Thank you for explaining."

I went on up to my bedroom while he was bowing and saying "Thank *you* for your understanding, madam."

I wondered if he'd be so relieved if he knew

what I thought I understood. Oh, he was unquestionably correct that Qeman was overflowing with friends, relatives, and family get-togethers. And remembering the toothy grin of Fatuoma's desert uncle and the mirth at his obviously salacious comment about the girl, I could believe that Nita's beauty might excite desire. It was kind of Ibrahim to include me . . . *but I didn't believe a word of it*.

For one thing, Azriel hadn't wanted us in the shop any more than Ibrahim did. For another, if there were anything really dangerous, he wouldn't have employed the two girls as ladies' maids, and he'd have told John to tell me to stay away. I remembered Ross's saying, "Maybe I want to go where they don't care for visitors." Coupled with Ian's Bedouin pal, Ibrahim's explanation was clever—but it was not clever enough. I lit a cigarette, stretched on the chaise longue with the last of my iced tea, and thought.

Azriel ibn-Ferid hadn't minded us at first; he'd settled happily to the normal leisurely bargaining. And although he had certainly kept a weather eye on my peregrinations, I realized now that this had been to spot whatever caught my attention, as a prelude to further sales. Then, suddenly, he'd become nervous. Of course, he couldn't be sure I understood no Arabic—but I'd been within earshot of the boys in the back room for some minutes before Azriel had begun to sweat.

Then he had rapidly concluded the bargaining, abandoned any future sales, and tried to get rid

of us. It was the voice. Azriel had recognized it;
and now it came back to me that the uproarious
greetings had started while I was considering the
runner for Mother. Lost in decision, I'd ignored
the racket behind the rug curtains. But for Azriel's
anxiety, egging me to awareness, I would never
have thought of it again.

Who was that man? Azriel knew he was someone connected with me, someone I ought to recognize. Already, in only a few hours' time, it was
hard to recall the exact tone. I'd thought of Gregor Semirov and monsieur Drouet—although I
found it hard to imagine the elderly suavity of
Henri swathed in native robes, skittering about
the native quarter of Qeman. Semirov, then? It
made sense, in a way.

Ibrahim made sense too—not as the voice itself,
but for the explanation. He might be on our side
over the contract, but he was still an Arab, and his
finger might be in any number of pies. If they
were unconnected with the Kennetts, he'd take
good care to separate me from any involvement. If
anything unpleasant happened to me or my guest,
he'd be in a very awkward position. The Palace
would lose face, leading to a catbird seat for John
and Mr. Baker on completion of contract terms—
and ending with the Sheikh's displeasure for his
distant cousin in whom he had reposed full confidence. I chuckled naughtily to myself, picturing
the dismay Ibrahim had shown when Fatuoma
and Zoe came bouncing into the servants' quarters
and revealed all!

I decided to tell John, for what it was worth in palaver-value, and let it go at that. I thought I wouldn't mention the voice, since I couldn't identify it, and by now I felt convinced that even though Azriel had feared I could, it had nothing to do with us. If, as Ross had said, that was where one arranged to take hush-hush trips, it would have been any one of the attachés on business quite unconnected with us.

At that point Nita stuck her head in the door. "He's gone," she announced, unnecessarily, "and I *may* have been wrong about its not working."

"Oh?"

"He's a bit more interested in *me*," she said, nodding, "but he's still cautious and unduly concerned with ˮBob—Who is he? Why's he here? How long will he stay? Et cetera. I said I didn't know, except he was an old friend of John's, and why shouldn't he be visiting? I'm visiting you, after all. Okay?"

"A-okay."

"I fixed the camel race. Ian's going to arrange a short trip to the nearest camp, with a Western-type barbecue for supper and a display of trick riding for Occidentals only. I'm booked to drive back with him and admire the stars. He says they're exceptional when viewed from the desert, and he'll enjoy giving me the Arabic names."

"Did you tell him you already passed Astronomy One?"

"Not me, darling," she protested, wide-eyed. "I've seen deserts, but not *Arabic* stars—always far

too closely chaperoned." She waggled her eyebrows at me blandly and started to turn away,
then turned back casually. "Oh, he doesn't want
us in that shop either. What is it—the local bor-
dello?"

"That makes three. Ibrahim was positively
stuffy about it. From what he said, I gather it's
the local dispatch point for white slaves."

She went off laughing—not that my evasion
fooled her, but one of Nita's greatest qualities is
"leave it alone unless it concerns you." You could
tell her anything and be sure it'd go no farther—or
you could tell her nothing by indirection and be
sure she'd faithfully spread whatever you wanted
her to spread. She'd be the perfect wife for anyone
hush-hush. I wondered sadly if she'd ever find a
man to replace Larry in her heart. *Damn* all these
wars and incidents—and now it looked as though
we might be in the middle of one here. For the first
time I felt uneasy at having dragged her into possible danger. Perhaps we should abandon the
whole thing, go to Lebanon, and let Fate play soli-
taire.

My husband and my friend were equally dear
to me; if anything happened to either of them, I'd
be a long time getting over it. I got up with a sigh.
The die was cast. She wouldn't leave unless I
came with her, and I wouldn't leave so long as
there was any chance of a random shot's hitting
John. Oh well; what will be, will be—and what
will not, will not. . . .

Ian encountered stiff competition that evening. First, Sir Percival pulled rank and swept Nita to the bridge tables, where she delighted him by skillfully making a grand slam that he never should have bidden in the first place, let alone redoubled. She then even more skillfully enchanted him by saying modestly, "Oh, give praise where it's due—a lot of the credit goes to you!" Then she asked earnestly whether, if she found a waltz record, he would dance with her—"because I think we should quit while we're ahead—don't you agree?" Old Perce was more jovial Old School Tie than ever under this flattering treatment. "No, no; you'll find better partners than I, m'gel—though I won't find anyone better than you—but go along, do. Somebody'll be willin' to cope with the old man."

Unfortunately, since I did not remove myself quickly enough, "somebody" turned out to be me, which was a fate worse than death. Sir Percival released all his diplomatically frustrated spirit of adventure in his bidding of bridge hands. No matter where he sat—East, West, North, or South—he was still a descendant of Sir Francis Drake, as he far too often informed us.

And since he'd apparently inherited the fruits of his ancestor's piracy, he could afford to be a lousy bridge player. The rest of us found Sir Percival's modern derring-do a bit hard on the budget. It was tacitly understood that we took turns partnering him. Tonight it should have been that Venezuelan girl whose name I could never remember, but somehow Bob had got me into Nita's seat and was sweeping her to the dance floor before Ian could step forward, so tonight was definitely going well for our side.

Apparently the other lads had ganged up to pay Ian back for last night's preemption of Nita. Since it was informal, introductions were not required, and from my seat (where I was taking the easy way out by sticking Old Perce to play every hand), I could see that the only person not permitted a full turn about the floor was Ian. He no sooner cut in than he was cut out, although everybody else was allowed a full dance. It even seemed as though Bob were the mastermind, right at hand to do most of the cutting. Ian was growing sulkier by the minute.

Unfortunately, I could also see John competing with Gregor for Sheila. Then I couldn't see him— for a full twenty minutes. Was she crying all over him in the garden? I am never the world's best bridge player, but I was more erratic than usual, until Sir Percival called me rather sharply to order—at which point I overbade him and proceeded to make an impossible contract in diamonds. With the recklessness of despair, I took deep finesses in every direction, ending with an overtrick and Sir Percival stuttering, "Fran, m'dear gel—brilliantly played, but how came you to bid diamonds when it was señor Marques's original suit?"

"Why shouldn't I?" I returned airily. "I made it, didn't I?"

"Yes; yes, you did—but heaven knows how."

"With the help of God and a long-handled spoon," I said absently, watching John and Sheila coming back from the garden. She was unobtrusively wiping her eyes, tucking the hanky in his breast pocket as they slid into the dance. "If that's the rubber, I think I've had enough. Can I get you another partner, Sir Percival?"

"No, thank you, m'dear. I think I've had enough too. Good heavens; you only had four trumps," he was muttering dazedly. "Holes in every suit . . ."

I was brazen enough to shrug and smile as though it was all the simplest thing in the world—although the plain truth was that I hadn't even heard señor Marques's original and had only bidden because I had a blank in spades and Sir Percival said, irascibly, "Your bid, I *think*, partner. What *is* the matter with you, Fran?"

By the time I got to the dance floor, Bob had relented and Ian was being allowed a noncut with Nita. Gregor had got Sheila, and John was on the sidelines watching them. "Oh, here you, Fran," he said unnecessarily, when I stood in front of him. "Care to dance?"

"Yes, please." I fitted myself into his arms, but it was evident that his mind wasn't on his feet. Neither was it on me. John is no Astaire even when trying. For some reason unknown to me, Princeton men are always better singers than dancers. We bumped and bucketed about the room, colliding painfully with other couples at every

turn, until finally I said, "Sir Perce has left—could
we go too?"

"Why?"

"It's been a longish sort of day. I took Nita
shopping, and she bought a rug," I said experi-
mentally. But apparently Ibrahim hadn't spoken
to him, because John merely agreed that bargaining was an exhausting business, and we'd go after
this dance. In a way, it confirmed my suspicion
that the rug shop was unconnected with the contract.

At that point, Bob cut Ian away from Nita, and
Ian went off to Sheila, moving rather unsteadily.
"C'mon; we're going." For once she made no protest beyond shrugging ungraciously, but John was
equally willing to leave—presumably because he
wouldn't get another dance with her. Once home,
he and Bob politely excused themselves and shut
the study door firmly. Nita and I went up to bed,
where she said, "Nothing to report, except he *talks*
more sex when he's stoned. I'm bushed, sweetie—
how about you?"

"Flat out. See you tomorrow, hon." I must have
gone to sleep as I hit the pillow. I never heard
John; he slept in his dressing room. I wondered
next day if he'd even opened my door before de-
ciding not to disturb me.

Formally clad for a tea party, we presented ourselves at the French Embassy, to be welcomed
heartily by madame Drouet, who stated impres-

sively that it was true—Henri would emerge! He
did, indeed—and in five seconds I knew he wasn't
the elusive voice. Before we left, it was confirmed.
Nita happened to ask how to ask for philatelic
supplies in Arabic, and despite Henri's fluency,
the timbre was more guttural, less whining.

But first we had iced lemonade flavored with
crème de cassis, flanked with superb *petits fours*.
Madame Drouet and Nita were charmed with
each other in a cascade of fluid French I could
understand, but never duplicate. I didn't try; I
spoke English, which they kindly accepted, until
Henri "emerged."

Primed beforehand, Nita conquered him immediately by describing her inherited collection. She
modestly confessed she was not adding to it,
merely preserving it for posterity—but if it con-
tained some prize monsieur Drouet yearned to
possess, she would gladly part with it (at market
value) to complete his collection. He was inclined
to shocked disapproval at separating a set of
stamps, but Nita widened her eyes ingenuously.
"Why not? It'll only go to a museum when I die—
and why shouldn't you have a few? You'll give
them a good home—and what becomes of your
collection when you're through with it?"

"It will go to the Philatelic Museum," he said
instantly.

"*Enfin.*" She shrugged. "*Sans doute* it will be
better to complete yours at the expense of mine,
if both go to museums, no?"

For the first time I could visualize the young

Henri Drouet. His supermarket-scallion appearance suddenly straightened up, his dark eyes sparkled with enthusiasm, his voice became vibrant—and in five minutes, he'd taken Nita away to his inner sanctum, there to view his treasures and list the gaps.

Berthe Drouet was different too. Her black eyes sparkled, but with affection. She practically purred with satisfaction to see her husband animated by a beautiful young woman. When we were alone, she went straight to the heart of the matter. "*Alors, chérie;* 'ow does it go? She is 'itting the nail on the top?"

"We don't know. We think he's being cautious, for fear of another transfer."

She nodded thoughtfully. "Yes, he is shrewd, *celui-ci. En effet,* he is neatly caught between the jealous wife, who may send him somewhere even less desirable than Qeman, and the beautiful rich woman, who is willing to flirt but is perhaps not willing to marry a man who is—'ow you say it?—on the skids."

For once she had it pat. We sipped lemonade silently for a moment. "I said I didn't think she'd ever leave him—but I'm beginning to think he wouldn't let her go either," I remarked.

"Ah? Why you say so?"

"It's only a feeling." I searched helplessly for words. "Why is he complaisant at her flirtations? If he really wanted out, from what you say, he could have got out long ago—and by now, she would be walking on eggs not to give him the least chance. Instead, here they are, still together. Maybe he likes a wife he can slap around; maybe he wants to be the big frog in a small puddle—and no rich woman would stand it for a second."

"I say it before—you are more smart than you know, *mignonne*."

"Not really, or I'd never have dragged Nita into it."

"*Oui;* there is that," she agreed. "*Vois-tu, ma petite;* it was never necessary. You will not lose your John, *je t'assure*. He is . . . 'aving a moment. All men 'ave them occasionally; one has only to wait. In the end, the eyes open, and they are thankful to *le bon Dieu* for the good wife that is so much better than the flirt." She squinted reflectively. "When it is over, you should ask for whatever you 'ave been wanting. A mink jacket, a diamond pin"—she shrugged—"whatever—'ow you say? Whatever the subway will carry."

"Whatever the traffic will bear," I murmured automatically.

"*Oui, c'est ça.* One looks at the bankbook and gauges the request accordingly. One says nothing of the incident, *naturellement*, but in the joy of being home once more, the husband buys the *petite desire* one has wistfully mentioned. That is always best," she stated parenthetically. "A man does not know how to economize on such matters, so one receives the best quality."

I thought fleetingly of madame Drouet's jewels and the sable evening wrap. It seemed *impossible* Henri could ever have been naughty enough to provide these "homecoming" presents, but perhaps he'd been more devilish in his youth. "Well, I wish you'd told me all this in the beginning, before I lit the fires," I fretted. "If you knew it wasn't necessary, why didn't you say so?"

"Because I am a wicked old woman," she sighed. "I think to myself it will be *amusante* to observe the progress of this affair. . . . At my age, after so many years in the diplomatic colonies, one has not much interest, *tu comprends?* Henri has his stamps; I have the people . . . but now, I wish also I had not encouraged you to invite your friend," she said soberly. "It would be wise for her to leave, and yes," as I opened my mouth, "I know she will not, unless you go with her. But"—she fixed me with a firm eye—"you are not to go again to Azriel's shop, Françoise!"

"No. But *why* not?"

"Because that is the headquarters of the nationalists," she said, surprised. "You did not know?"

I shook my head, but before I could explore the matter, Nita and monsieur Drouet were "emerging." We left shortly afterward. Henri had retreated once more, and madame Drouet patted Nita's hand softly. "Thank you for giving such pleasure to my 'usband, *ma chère*. He 'as not much to amuse him. It was kind in you."

"I enjoyed it," Nita said sincerely. "His collection is magnificent. It was kind of you to let us come, madame. I'm always happy to meet the people Fran likes."

"Ah, it is good to see friendship among women,

but you understan' . . . it will not be pretty when the explosion arrive?" madame Drouet warned. "*Moi qui vous parle*, I can tell you Mrs. 'Aysrath is a tigress. She slaps, she bites, she scratches *Prenez garde*, ma'amselle!"

Nita raised her eyebrows. "Ah, so? Thanks for the briefing, but I'm a tigress myself where Fran is concerned."

There was a message from John when we reached home—He and Bob would be delayed. Would we go alone, and they'd pick us up later? Ibrahim delivered the message expressionlessly, and Nita looked at me. "Where were we supposed to be?"

"Dessert and coffee at the Peruvians', I think."

"The Chileans', madam." Ibrahim stared into space.

"Same difference," Nita said. "*Must* we go, Fran? Couldn't we get comfortable and stay home for a change?"

"Of course. Ibrahim, please telephone and say, uh . . . Miss Janus has the botts."

"And we are canceling all engagements until the vermifuge works," she added swiftly. "Come, Fran."

I looked back from the upper hall. Ibrahim was staring after us with the effect of being open-mouthed, although his face was motionless as always. I smiled at him blandly and went away to my bedroom. Was it our levity, or was botts unknown in The Yard? Heaven knows what he told the Chileans, but when Nita and I came down in housecoats, drinks were waiting on the patio. Later dinner appeared, accompanied by candlelight and a bowl of fragile floating lotus blossoms. "Where's Fouad?" I asked, as Ibrahim set jellied consommé before me.

"It is his free day, madam."

"I suppose it's too much to hope he's using the time to take a bath," Nita observed outrageously. But on top of botts, we couldn't hope for any reaction. Ibrahim merely set a wicker basket of crackers between us, and removed himself. Austerely. Nita looked after him until he'd vanished into the kitchen. "Wherever did he learn this? D'you suppose he had to wait table in Commons? It seems a bit demeaning for a relative of His Highness—"

"Quit it," I muttered warningly. "You're not supposed to know anything—and anyway, Commons is Princeton."

"So it is; I'd forgotten . . . which reminds me, d'you remember Sue Machem? She's running the most fabulously successful string of suburban eateries. . . ."

We were still lazing over coffee and reminiscence when the boys came back. John looked a bit disconcerted at finding us there, instead of monkeying around a dance floor. For a moment, he was rather of the opinion that we should get dressed and put in an appearance for one dance.

"Oh, nonsense," said Bob, fixing a drink and

sinking down beside Nita with a deep sigh. "If you haven't had it for today, you're a glutton for punishment. Personally, bless the girls for getting us out of it!"

John hesitated, and despite madame Drouet's heartening analysis, I couldn't help wondering if he'd looked forward to dancing with Sheila. But finally he said, "You're right. I'm so used to the treadmill, I can't belive in reprieve."

We wound up playing a spirited game of Monopoly, with a complete new set of rules figured out by Nita and Bob. Everything was sheer extortion and usury. We laughed so much we could hardly play—except John, who kept his mind on things and eventually wiped us all out.

Bob figured it out over a nightcap. "I make it four million I owe you, plus the Empire State Building," he said finally. "D'you mind a check, old man? I'm a little short of cash tonight—forgot to go to the bank this morning."

As Nita had said, Bob was rather a dear. John was looking infinitely better, relaxing, lounging comfortably in his chair. It was exactly the kind of evening he needed. We were in bed by eleven, for a change, and John was in my room instead of the dressing room—although he was asleep before I finished brushing my teeth.

All the same, it was reassuring to hear his even breathing in the darkness . . .

An hour later, we were awakened by pattering footsteps and a shadowy figure flitting along the gallery past the bedroom windows.

* * *

Ibrahim had sensed the intruder in the study, but for all his speed, the man escaped through the window to the outside stairs, then around the gallery to the other side of the house, where he slithered down a palm tree to the street beyond the wall. He was long gone by the time John and Bob had thrown on bathrobes and joined Ibrahim at the railing. Through the open window I could hear them returning while I struggled into a negligee. "He wore Arab clothing," Ibrahim was saying quietly, "but I do not think he was Arab, Mr. Kennett."

I met Nita in the hall. "What's going on?"

There was nothing for it but to tell her. "Someone broke in. It's the oil negotiations, been going on for weeks." I hurried down the stairs, with Nita right behind me. "Someone's trying to find out the terms of the agreements and stir up trouble."

"Oh. That's why Ibrahim and Bob. I thought as much."

The study was in wild confusion, but the contract had not been found. John said merely that he didn't have a copy and wouldn't have kept it in the study in any case. He had his hand on the telephone, when it rang. We could all hear Baker's agitated voice. "Kennett, you okay? I've had a search here. . . ."

"So have we. He didn't get anything—just upset the place a bit."

I tugged at Nita's sleeve, and we faded away tactfully, to sit in the lounge until John was finished. For once she asked a few questions, and I gave her a tailored version of events, still omitting mention of Elvig's murder. "Why didn't you tell me before?" she inquired.

"I thought it might frighten you." I shrugged. "And it's no concern of yours, after all."

"I was never frightened of anything in my life, and you know it," she retorted, "and it *is* my concern if you've involved." Before she could say another word, John and Bob came in.

"He didn't get anything at Baker's—that's if it was the same person."

"It was," Nita said promptly.

"How do you know?" Bob asked quietly.

"Use your head! We weren't supposed to be here—we were supposed to be at the Chileans'. And I guess Mr. Baker went?" Bob nodded, his eyes steadily fixed on her. Nita shrugged. "So whoever it is hit Baker first. Because he's upper echelon, he'd leave with Sir Percival, and we'd be expected to stay for another dance or two. When he didn't find what he wanted, he came here—and it looked as though we hadn't got home, whereas we were already in bed."

"Very sound reasoning," Bob approved.

"That argues it wasn't someone who could go to the party," I remarked, "or he'd have known we weren't there."

"Yes, but we might have been elsewhere. Baker says it was all youngsters; the Dutch Ambassador was rank. It wasn't intended to be a big party; not everyone was asked, because the Spaniards in-

vited the older group for coffee and bridge," John
said absently. "Baker stayed long enough for a
few dances, and when Vandam gave him the high
sign, they went on to Marques's, and everybody
was there, playing roulette as well as bridge. So
you see, for all anyone would know, we could all
have been there, if our house was dark."

"Well, if he didn't get anything, it's all right," I
said, but the men were looking much more worried than seemed warranted.

"You don't understand, Fran. It's not that an attempt was made—but how did the fellow get in?
The servants were gone for the night, and Bob
and I made sure everything was secured before
we went to bed. Nothing's forced. It's the same at
Baker's—study rifled but nothing forced." John
ran a hand through his hair wearily. "Someone's
got a key."

We sat silent, considering the implications.
"The Russians?" I asked. "It seems the sort of
thing they'd do."

"Perhaps."

"Shouldn't you have the locks changed tomorrow?"

"They *were* changed," John said grimly. "Ibrahim got a man down from Basra."

We thought *that* one over, until Nita said,
"Well, call it the Case of the Revolving Locks, and
have 'em changed every hour on the half hour. If
you can't afford it, I can—and we'll call it my
house present. I'd been wondering what to give
you."

· "It's not a bad idea," Bob announced unexpectedly. "Get a selection of lock barrels from Cairo and Athens, John; we can put them in ourselves. That'll slow future attempts, at least."

"Dear me, how exciting this is," Nita observed. "I wish you'd told me I was coming into an international spy ring, Fran. I'd have brought some disguises so I could play too."

The thought of Nita in a blond wig and spectacles provided just the light note we needed. Still laughing, we trooped back to bed, and in the bright sunlight next morning, the whole thing seemed grotesque.

Three days later I found the contract. . . .

8

It was tucked beneath a small pile of winter woollies, which I had optimistically brought on the
chance there'd be time for a vacation before
John's next assignment. After a succession of hot
climates, a cruise in the Norwegian fjords seemed
indicated for a change of pace. By rights, I should
never have found the thing. This was the storage
chest for everything else, the basic stuff to use for
unlikely moments—things like plastic raincoats,
folding rubbers, and heavy sweaters for cold
countries—or conversely, if it's cold where you are,
lightweight sportshirts, bathing togs, and espa-
drilles.

Also props. The Belgian had decreed a costume
party for next week. This is a major hazard in foreign colony society. Somebody always becomes
desperate for entertainment and decides to let the
guests amuse each other. In five years, I'd ac-
quired the equipment for turning John into a pi-
rate, a Rough Rider (same hat, take off the skull
and crossbones), and a Minister without Portfolio
(a tasty selection of pawn-shop medals plus two

yards of red ribbon across the chest under his dinner jacket). Similarly, I could be a Spanish dancer (silk rose and shawl), or an odalisque (satin pants of my lounging pajamas, with spangled nose veil). I hadn't been able to portray Mary Pickford since someone's tame wombat got out of its cage in Kenya and ate the wig I'd combed, curled, and hung out to air.

I didn't find the box of rhinestones or the bogus tiara I wanted for Nita—but as I rummaged about, I heard a crackling noise. From the bottom of the drawer, I drew out a wad of legal paper, neatly folded. A single glance told me what it was—two copies—one English, one Arabic. "An Agreement between His Highness Sulieman Ali ibn-Feisal, Sheikh of Qeman, etc. . . ." I didn't go any farther. Quite apart from my inability to make sense of the legal language, some inner caution whispered, "What you don't know, you can't tell." I refolded the documents and sat cross-legged on the floor, gulping in remembered fright at the searcher who'd left the study in turmoil. And all the time what he wanted had been secreted among my winter underwear.

It was logical that John must have put the contract in this drawer. I could spare an admiring thought for his superb aplomb that night when he had said without a quiver that of course he didn't have the contract. I remembered, further, that he'd said he wouldn't have kept it in the study anyway—and *that* was the truth, I thought angrily, when he knew damn well it was in my storage

chest. For a moment I was furious at such duplicity, such carelessness—until it struck me that
whoever had a key to our house could probably
open a safe, as well.

Perhaps it wasn't so dumb after all. The search
of my rooms had ceased weeks ago, and there
must never have been any sign of search elsewhere in the house or Ibrahim would have spotted
it. I was still convinced that the darkroom incident had been tied to Ross Elvig. Once the intruder was convinced I didn't have his films, I was
undisturbed. At the time, I had been so annoyed by
the clumsy waste of materials that I'd bought a
combination padlock at the European hardware
store, stood over Fouad while he attached the steel
bar, and made certain the screws were tight as soon
as he'd gone. Ever since, the darkroom had been
open only when I was *in* it; I locked it even if I
stepped out only to go to the bathroom.

I thought now that it might be a better hiding-
place than a bottom drawer—but if someone had
bribed the locksmith from Basra, the number of
my lock might also be known. Although I'd seen
no trace, it might be regularly inspected by someone more skillful, who merely observed without
touching and, on identifying my pictures as local
scenery, left them alone.

In any case, I couldn't take chances. John had
put the contract in the drawer; if I moved it and
he found it gone before I could alert him, he'd
probably never speak to me again for giving him
such a shock. I replaced the papers, pulling the

woollies securely over them, and decided to *suggest* the darkroom. Let him make up his own mind. It wouldn't be long now, anyway. Tonight was the end of Ramadan. Tomorrow the Sheikh would get back to the bargaining table. In a day or so, once the holiday strangers had left Qeman, he'd be ready to sign—if nothing occurred to upset the applecart while the town was still crammed to bursting with Qemani ready to whoop it up after a month of religion.

I shivered slightly. The place was a tinderbox at this moment. Any repetition of the fracas from which Ibrahim had saved me would develop into a full-scale riot. Good Moslems are teetotalers; not all Arabs are good Moslems. Very quietly I shut the drawer, crept to the door, and reconnoitered, but the house was entirely still, enjoying siesta. I slid along to my own room, apparently unobserved, and closed the door with a sigh of relief. I was just in time; siesta was ending in a series of faint movements, soft voices in the rear yard . . . and Ian Haysrath, in the lower hall, asking for Miss Janus.

"I will inquire, sir. . . ."

I'd left Nita on the patio while I went up to look for the rhinestones. In a minute, I could hear Ibrahim saying, "This way, sir." More than ever, I wished I hadn't asked her to visit. Ending John's possible romantic involvement with Sheila was no longer so important as keeping Nita safe. Why, *why* hadn't I left well enough alone? Because I was a stupid, temperish, jealous fool, that's why.

Unnerved by discovering that damned contract and finally realizing the very present danger that surrounded all of us, I swung mentally vice versa. *Let* John be heartbroken if Sheila wouldn't have him—or *let* him divorce me to marry a miserable housekeeper. I'd go back to Toledo and find another husband who'd be glad to have babies *at once!*

I'd worked myself into a lather by the time Fatuoma came in to prepare for the evening—and it was going to be an important evening, I remembered with a sinking heart. Mr. Baker was giving a formal reception and dinner, to mark the end of Ramadan. There was to be a package deal of Americans on an international cultural-exchange tour, persuaded to stop over in Qeman en route from Israel to India. Madame Iandouros would wear the sapphires, signora Francia would display rubies, Tomyienkov would be a classless sausage in her bronze taffeta, and madame Drouet would . . . well, you could never tell *what* she'd be. Nita could wear anything and look beautiful. What about me?"

"Fatuoma, tonight I will wear the white dress you cleaned for me."

Her face lit up. "Yes; is correct," she said eagerly. "You want pretty bag?"

"Bag?"

"Yes; I keep for you."

My face must have shown instinctive revulsion, for she said quietly, "Not stained; is perfect. I keep so you not remember and cry."

"Thank you, Fatuoma. Yes; I'd like the bag."

I was bathed, half-dressed, and keeping one ear alert for sounds of John when Nita finally came upstairs. "He insisted on having drinks, Fran, so I let him. D'you mind? I thought it might soften him up, and it did. We're booked for a private viewing of the moon over the desert next week—just we two, alone under the stars, unbeknownst to anyone. A sort of trial elopement, I gather."

"Oh, dear—I wish I hadn't got you into this, Nita."

"Nonsense," she said. "It's exactly what's wanted. As soon as it's definitely dated, you will drop a word, which will instantly reach her ears—I've encountered grapevines, but I never saw *anything* like Qeman before—and we can expect the eruption in time to prevent my fate worse than death. Simple, my dear Watson." She shrugged lightly and went off to have her bath. I could hear her whistling the Habanera, with great emphasis on *"Prends garde à toi."*

What I couldn't hear was John, although time was growing short and he should have been in his dressing room.

I'd finished my makeup before there was any sound. I flung open the door relievedly and said, "John, thank goodness—" But it was only Ibrahim. He turned away swiftly, while I removed my unclad form with equal speed. "I beg your pardon, madam. Mr. Kennett and Colonel Penniston are dressing at Mr. Baker's—I took over their clothes personally. Fatuoma was instructed to tell you."

"Oh, dear, I expect she tried, Ibrahim, but I didn't understand her."

It was true, she'd been fluttering about, saying "Mr. Kennett . . ." and I'd thought she was merely trying to tell me John would be proud of me in the white dress. I said, "Well, thank you, Ibrahim," and retreated—to find Fatuoma waiting to slide the dress over me and drape a towel about my shoulders until I'd arranged my hair. I sat down before the dressing table—and the white evening bag lay silently staring at me.

She was right that it was unstained; it was also still full of whatever I'd had that evening, which presumably was the usual complement of hanky, cigarettes, compact, and so on. Like most women, the evening bags in my modest assortment have gradually become equipped, so that one only adds cigarettes and a fresh handkerchief. In consequence, I hadn't missed or needed the contents of this one in the interval since Ross's death. Tentatively, I picked it up and opened. If there were cigarettes, they'd be abominably stale by now. It felt oddly heavy to my hand. Involuntarily I upended the thing, spilling the contents onto the dressing table.

The last items to emerge were four small rolls of film.

I twitched the hanky over them and said, "Fatuoma, please ask Zoe if Miss Janus is dressed." When she'd obediently gone out of the room, I removed the handkerchief and stared at the films with a shiver working uncontrollably up my spine.

Ross's, of course—the ones they couldn't find, that *Life* had said must exist. He'd stuffed them into my bag when I dropped it that evening—when he muttered, "Meet me," and when I'd caught Henri Drouet's sharp glance and wondered if he could read lips. . . .

I no longer thought he was our spy—but someone had been certain I had those films. Someone had hit Fatuoma and searched the darkroom. Someone had only been convinced by my genuine innocent bewilderment . . . And all the time, the films were in an evening bag Fatuoma had kindly removed, to spare me a distressing memory!

By rights the films should go to Gerson or to *Life* Magazine, and the hell with ethics. I had the lock off the darkroom door and the films inside and was preparing the pans when Fatuoma came back. "Mees will be ready—" she began, and shrieked faintly at sight of me. "No, no, no, take off dress *first!*" I let her unzip me and set the dress back on its hanger before I vanished again. While I dissolved and stirred, I thought fleetingly that her reaction was delightful. Apparently nothing, to Fatuoma, could be more natural than for Madam Kennett to decide to work in her darkroom after being completely dressed for a formal evening! I wondered, with sudden anxiety, if she'd report this madness to the other servants. A calculated risk, I decided, opening one reel after another with steady fingers and spooling the film strips into my Nikor reels. Somehow I knew that despite her uncle's connection with nationalists,

Fatuoma was no gossip. For one thing, if she were anything but what she seemed—an honest, uncomplicated youngster—I would not now have Ross Elvig's films.

It would have been logical for her to open my bag, if only to look at the compact and lipstick case; logical for her to tell someone innocently of the unusual extras not normally found in an evening bag. She had not. She had done what she said—removed the bag for fear of distressing me, and faithfully kept it without even looking inside. If she had so much as mentioned a bag, someone would have examined it and removed the film— even Ibrahim. No; Fatuoma had said nothing. It was unlikely she'd speak of this, either.

There wouldn't be time for prints, but at least I'd have the negatives, and I might be able to read them well enough to know why Ross had had to be killed. "Dear Lord, let me not make a mistake!" Ross had been willing to let me develop for him— the mere fact that he'd jettisoned the film into my evening bag showed he felt he could rely on me. That was heartening. Of course, he hadn't expected to be knifed; he might have expected to retrieve the reels and develop them himself.

I sat in my underslip, carefully transferring the reels from the developer to the stop bath, and then to the fixer, and feeling an almost superstitious responsibility. For the first time in weeks, I let myself remember Ross Elvig. If he were alive today, I knew I still wouldn't really like him. I'd still think him brash, brassy, pushing—and yet . . .

There are lots of people you don't much care for, but you won't clap hands if they're *murdered*.

The final strip was fixed and in the wash water, and Fatuoma was tapping on the door. "Madam Kennett, Mees Janus ready."

"Tell her five minutes. . . ."

"Selim ready too," she said warningly. "Is time; come quick you can."

"Five minutes, Fatuoma."

I think she must have watched the clock, for just as I was taking the negatives from the wash, she was at the door again. "Please, is still dress . . . hair . . . pretty pearls," she wailed distractedly. "Ibrahim not like you late; blame me. Please?"

"Yes; all right, I'm coming." I pulled the final reel from the wash, unspooled the film, clipped it alongside its companions, and attached the bottom weight. The last thing I wanted was any need for an explanation by Fatuoma to Ibrahim for my delay, but she was entirely satisfied when I emerged. In a twinkling she had me zipped into my dress once more and was sighing with relief that my hair and makeup needed no retouching. I *had* to get rid of her for long enough to examine the negatives. "Fatuoma, run quickly—bring me a glass of iced tea, while I put on my earrings?"

She was gone in a flash, and instantly I was in the darkroom, peering at the damp film strips, to find—*nothing!* I held them to the light and turned them this way and that, but if they held any clue to Ross's murderer, it couldn't be read from the tiny frames. They seemed no more than he'd originally said—pictures of a desert camp. There were tents, camels, groups of men about a fire over which hung a spitted lamb. But on thirty-five-millimeter film, you'd need a magnifying glass to identify faces. Just one seemed familiar—a close-up of two men, laughing heartily. I wasn't certain, but it might be Fatuoma's desert uncle. There was a dark patch in his open mouth that might be a gold tooth. The other man was simply another native, bearded and swathed in white robes.

I hung the negatives back on the hooks, feeling more depressed than ever in my life. Logically, there *had* to be something here, something Ross had thought dangerous enough to secrete it in my bag, something for which he'd been killed. I'd locked the darkroom and was fussing at the dressing table again, when Fatuoma panted in with the cold drink—and I needed it. I drank it down in a series of grateful gulps and determinedly abandoned all thought of Ross Elvig. Tomorrow would tell the tale. Then, I could print the films—if they were still here.

I gambled that Fatuoma would say nothing of the darkroom, but for once, I did not say, "Don't wait up for me." That should ensure an innocent guardian for the films until I got back.

"Can I help?" Nita asked quietly, in the silence of the car.

"No; it's go for broke—but cross everything you've got, including your eyes." I glanced warningly at Selim; he mightn't speak much English, but that was no guarantee he didn't understand more than he spoke. She nodded and said no more, while I seethed impatiently. The instant we reached Baker's house, I had to get John alone and tell him what I'd found, ask whether we dared leave the films, or should he tell Ibrahim to be on guard . . . or something.

I was frustrated on all counts. Never had it taken so long to get to Bêt Americano, and it was entirely my own fault. If I hadn't delayed us to develop the films, we'd have started that much earlier; now it was after sundown, Ramadan was offically ended, and the streets were already clogged with happy Arabs, camels, goats, and native stalls selling sweetmeats or fruit. It should have been a memorable scene, vividly colorful. Nita was absorbing it wholeheartedly; I couldn't share her pleasure, with Selim slowed to a crawl, occasionally stopped dead until a way was cleared for our car. And when we finally got to Baker's, the reception was well under way. I had hoped to catch John in the room Baker had given him for late nights; instead, he and Bob were already dressed, downstairs in the thick of the crowd, so that was no good. The last thing I wanted was any hint of difference, to raise questions in someone's mind. *Wonder why Fran wanted to see John alone. . . . What could have happened?* . . .

He chanced to look up and see us arriving, and I tried beckoning. I thought that might seem unremarkable enough. I hadn't see him all day; it was natural to give him a kiss now; Americans are always affectionate in public. If I could just whisper, "Urgent, get away to your room" . . . It almost worked. His face lit up, he was beginning to worm through the crowd toward me, and that damned Sheila caught his hand, dragging him into a group. He stopped at once, of course, merely waving and nodding to me. He had no reason to think my summons was more than what I'd meant it to appear, but I didn't dare another beckon. A second try would be—unusual. Bob had reached the entry hall and was smiling appreciatively at Nita—I'd tell *him* to get John upstairs, or come himself. It would be safe enough to tell Bob. . . .

A swirl of new arrivals cut me off. Before I could reach the stairs, Nita was going up and Bob was receding to the reception room again. If only I'd told Nita I had to get word to John or Bob privately, she'd just had exactly the casual chance I was wanting. Inwardly raging at fate, I followed her up to the cloakroom.

It was crowded with women, chattering animatedly and taking turns for a final glance in the long mirror, a last check of hair and lipstick—and the moment I entered, the voices stopped with the effect of turning off a spigot. A second later, the conversation resumed, but it was obviously random, to cover gossip about—what? John and Sheila? Nita's eyes met mine inscrutably in the mirror. Whatever she'd overheard, she was giving nothing away.

I handed my wrap to the maid and allowed myself to be warmly greeted by a dozen women (was their friendliness a cover for pity?) and before I could get to Nita, she'd left the mirror. "See you downstairs, sweetie."

"Oh, *wait* for me!"

She lingered by the door—and madame Drouet detained me with a compelling hand. "*Alors*, you 'ave 'ad a burglar," she stated softly, and I was startled by the deadly seriousness of her black eyes. "A word of advice, *chèrie*—it is not good for men to 'ave to think of women in peril. So, you will come to me at any hour, *tous deux. C'est compris?*"

Over her head I could see Nita being inexorably pushed away from her waiting position by the influx of later guests. She raised her eyebrows, shrugged helplessly, and vanished downstream. "Yes; I understand, and thank you, madame Drouet."

She brushed aside my words. "Henri agrees—*at any hour*," she repeated, holding my eyes authoritatively. "Remember, Françoise!" I nodded silently, and she released my arm, to bend toward the mirror. I was literally shaking with fright as the crowd swept me to the door. It was not surprising that madame Drouet knew of the abortive burglary; she always knew everything within twenty minutes, or so it seemed. . . . And as easily as anyone else in Qeman she'd know the *raison d'être* . . . but what more did she know or suspect? For once, she was warning, grave, and protective. Without egotism, I knew she was fond of me; if it did not interfere with her husband, she would not wish harm to come to me—or to Nita, who'd amused him for an afternoon.

Going a step at a time through the crush on the stairs, I could see him gracefully kissing Nita's hand. Henri agreed we should make tracks for the French Embassy at any hour. . . . Henri was a fanatic philatelist, and Nita had some goodies he wanted. . . . Henri had "emerged" at a crucial moment. . . . Henri was shortly due to retire. It made a vague sequence in my mind, as I moved along.

There could be innocent explanations for everything. Henri did "emerge" occasionally, for top-notch affairs, of which tonight would definitely be one. If his long years in diplomacy led him to smell a dangerous situation, he'd undoubtedly tell his wife to get Nita out of it—at least until he could put his hands on her stamps. And I would have to come too, like a package deal.

Conversely, he might know that the situation was dangerous because he'd created it—and he'd still want Nita's stamps. He might have plunged into some undercover activity because he was retiring and hoped to make a coup for retirement income. He wasn't the man in Azriel's back room, but Berthe Drouet's immediate knowledge of backstairs gossip in Qeman argued a native pipe-line—and the voice might belong to one of the attachés who escorted her when Henri did not "emerge."

I'd reached the bottom of the stairs, worming politely through the crush. I couldn't see Henri as a master spy, somehow. It was not impossible but highly unlikely that a man universally respected throughout a long career would suddenly go off the rails. Vaguely, I thought I remembered someone—was it Sheila?—saying Drouet had private means.

"Madame Kennett . . . or may I be permitted to call you Françoise too?"

"I should be honored, monsieur Drouet." I looked at the keen eyes above his conventional smile and wondered fancifully what Henri would say if I asked, very calmly and conversationally, "Do tell me—who is this spy?" I had a peculiar certainty that both he and his wife *knew*, that if it weren't settled quickly, she would give me a clue. Perhaps she already had and I'd been too dumb to get it.

My face must have shown indecision, uncertainty, trouble, because Henri murmured, "*Soyez tranquille, ma chère Françoise;* it is unimportant; it will soon be finished." I smiled politely, while his glance slid toward John and Sheila, cozily ensconced in the farthest window seat. Well, that may have been what monsieur Drouet meant, but I didn't believe it. His expression was kindly, yet still reserved. Impulsively, I opened my mouth to say, "Please, help me . . ." and Gregor Semirov was at my elbow.

"Good evening. Where's your beautiful friend, Fran? I hear she shares your enthusiasm for stamps, monsieur Drouet."

"No, she does not. She has an inherited collec-

tion, and she was kind enough to tell me about it,
that's all." Monsieur Drouet shrugged humor-
ously. "We think she may have a few specimens to
complete certain series of mine—if I can afford
them."

Gregor smiled a bit wickedly. "You will, monsieur Drouet; you will," he prophesied, "even if
you have to sell your wife's jewels."

"Ah, you know me too well, Gregor," the
French Ambassador sighed sadly, "but I think it
will not come to that. Miss Janus does not have a
Penny Black nor the elusive Mauritius."

"But she does have that Bosnian Rose you were
wanting," I remarked with a grin. The moment for
confidence was gone, and probably just as well.
I'd been temporarily undermined by his friendliness, but he was still an unknown quantity. I *must*
reach John.

I couldn't.

It was a repetition of the night I'd wanted to
speak privately with Ross. No matter how I fina-
gled, I couldn't get free of people—or if I did,
John was surrounded. I suppose parties are always
like this, but it had never mattered before. Slowly,
the reception line snaked along, shaking hands
with the stars of the cultural exchange tour who
would entertain us later. Mr. Baker was looking
immensely jovial and pleased with himself, but
even when he kissed me heartily, Gregor was too
close for me to dare a whisper. Once finished with
formality, there were drinks and canapés, light
polite chit-chat, smiles and compliments "Your

dress is ravishing, madame. Ah, you have a new coiffure; it's most successful!"

"*Pourquoi tu est triste ce soir?*" Madame Drouet purred in my ear. "*Ne t-en fâche pas, chérie.* Enjoy the party!"

Granted she had X-ray eyes, if madame Drouet had noted my abstraction, others would shortly follow. *Mustn't permit the least hint of anything unusual—even if it's ascribed to marital difficulties.* I gritted my teeth mentally and abandoned myself to "What is to be, will, and what isn't, will not." I might be convinced that those negatives, once printed, would identify Ross's murderer. Perhaps the criminal wasn't meant to be caught? If I found the things gone when I got home, I'd say, "It was the will of Allah."

Meanwhile I joined the party in spirit as well as body. It was evidently going to be a major bim-bambasheroo, now that I could evaluate it. Aside from Mrs. Tomyienkov and myself, every woman in the place had a new dress. I found this distinctly lowering to the mind for a few minutes, until I persuaded myself that capitalism is as capable of economy as Communism, and on the whole we're still ahead. Tonight, madame Iandouros was exhibiting her back. There was almost as much of it as her front, though differently distributed; grape-colored silk came up to her chin before, and down to the waist behind. For one frivolous moment, I wondered if she'd got the gown on back-to-front, but perhaps she'd realized that frontal exposure was an old story by now. Anyway, her diamond necklace would not have been displayed to equal advantage against white skin.

Signora Francia wore white lace, with sapphires. Madame Drouet was stuffed into palest pink *peau d'ange*, with rubies . . . leading to the fascinating suspicion that they'd merely bought new dresses and exchanged their parures for the occasion.

Nita's clinging silk of immense pale gold chrysanthemums on white wasn't new; she'd got it three years ago from Balenciaga. Her jewelry was only an antique necklace of gold chains set with pearls peridots, of no special value. She possessed a few good jewels "for emergencies," as she put it, but she never traveled with them. The one time her small jewel case was stolen from a hotel in Lisbon, the thief later returned it—contemptuously intact.

That Venezuelan girl whose name I couldn't remember was sporting a few fabulous emeralds above lemon-yellow chiffon. Since she wasn't married, hence in madam Drouet's minor-blackmail league, I wondered whether they were a *preuve d'amour* or smuggled. Colombia controls emerald exports with a firm hand—but Venezuela is next-door, so to speak.

Even Sheila had a new dress, although after a second glance, I decided it was probably just new to me. It was hard to believe anyone would *buy* such a depressed acid-pink confection; in fact, I thought it was something run up by a native dressmaker in Afghanistan—but perhaps I'd have been more appreciative if she had not been sitting so close to John.

The rooms were jam-packed by now, and the men were nearly as colorful as the women. Red and blue ribbons, tiny lapel buttons, and sparkling decorations adorned dinner jackets, interspersed with dress uniforms loaded with gold braid and campaign stripes. Even Ian had some sort of small medal on his lapel. He was glued to Nita's side, looking wickedly handsome. If he'd been tiddly when he left her earlier, he was quite sober now, although there was a recklessness in his behavior. . . .

In contrast to all this glittering glamor, John's unadorned dinner suit seemed more or less mufti.

After a second highball, I felt much more party-ish . . . and suddenly, *directly behind me, I heard the voice in Azriel's shop*—or I thought I did. Whirling around, I faced Gregor, Sir Percival, signor Francia, and Mr. Iandouros, standing about Ian and Nita. A native servant was just moving away with his tray of drinks. Clearly, one of these men had spoken to him in Arabic, no more than a brief sentence, but recognizable because of the intonation. Now they were all speaking English again, and the timbres were not the same.

Logically, one of the men had asked for a fresh drink—but *all* the glasses were full. I'd ruled Ian out, but now he was in again, because it had to be one of this group. They all spoke fluent Arabic and were part of the group I knew best, and Azriel had been certain I knew that voice. It

seemed incredible to picture the English, Greek,
or Italian Ambassadors flitting about at night, rifling our studies! But Ross Elvig had been killed
at the Italian Embassy, and many Greeks are more
loyal to the Middle East than to Uncle Sam. I suppose it was instinctive prejudice—I still settled for
Gregor. John said the Russians didn't fit; as a
choice between Old Perce and Gregor, I thought
they'd fit better than the elderly deaf Englishman,
but the only way to be sure was to get Gregor to
say something in Arabic.

Apparently I'd have the chance, if I could be
subtle enough. When dinner was announced, Gregor presented himself to take me in. Protocol put
Sheila on his right, beside John, with Nita, Ian,
that dratted Venezuelan girl, and full circle with
Bob to my left. I only hoped I could get through
dinner without making a slip. A second highball
had given me Dutch courage, but was all too
likely to fuddle me as soon as we hit warm food.

Our burglar couldn't be ignored, nor was there
any longer a point in denying what, presumably,
he sought. Nita said it was a new thrill and deli-
ciously suspenseful. Sheila shuddered dramati-
cally, and whined that she'd always expected
something horrid in this awful hole. "If," she informed Nita, "you'd ever been through a native
riot, you wouldn't be so gay about having to be
locked into the houses, never knowing from one
moment to the next if the servants would turn
against you."

"Oh, is it likely to come to that?" Nita returned

coolly. "I thought the police looked unusually alert, and Sheikh Sulieman has an excellent reputation for keeping a firm hand on his country." She'd nearly deflected the conversation, as Sheila flared up stubbornly, citing so many instances of riot, arson, and sudden death that Nita was wide-eyed.

"Heavens! I had no notion diplomacy was so dangerous. Haven't you ever been posted anywhere but among cannibals and head-hunters?"

Sheila flushed angrily. Unexpectedly, the Venezuelan girl backed her up. "Do not joke," she observed somberly. "Caracas is one of the wealthiest, most sophisticated cities in the world, and no more than a picnic drive into the hills there are the Motilones. The big oil companies must pay double or triple to the pipeline surveyors. The governments of Colombia and Venezuela do their best, but it is still very wild country. Every so often"—she shrugged casually—"a survey camp is wiped out by a foray of the Motilones—when they are hungry." In the minute of silence about our table, she laid down her fish fork, wiped her fingers daintily, and sighed. "It is always good to dine at the Americans'," she remarked conversationally. "Everywhere in the world, the food is exceptional. Where come these shrimps not to be had locally? Delicious!"

"Flown in—frozen, of course, but shrimps are the one shellfish that survives edibly," I said swiftly. "Always good, any way at all, but a sauce makes them even better, don't you agree?"

"Yes." She nodded vehemently. "One can do anything with shrimps; lobster, also, but crab . . ."

"It has to be fresh," Nita agreed. "What sort of shellfish do you have in Venezuela?"

While they talked this over exhaustively, I managed to finish my shrimps, but I'd relaxed too soon. Gregor got us back to the damned contract, by asking about the Motilone Indians. Anna (I gathered that was her first name) explained they were a jungle tribe. "If it is a bad year, not enough corn in the villages, they revert to cannibalism—and afterward they shrink the heads and sell them as curios. Against the law, but one can always buy a shrunken head, and it is *not* the fault of the authorities. Short of sending an army into those hills and jungles and wiping out every Motilone, it's not possible to protect prospectors."

"I should say they've no business to be there in the first place," Gregor murmured. "Surely, these big corporations must know whether or not the harvest was good or bad? Why should they schedule a survey at such times?"

"For the same reason the Sheikh of Qeman's police force does nothing to prevent native burglaries," Ian said indolently. "One must always remember *he* is the intruder . . . not the native who is fired with a desire to see his country rich and respected. Misguided, perhaps, but understandable, to be reckoned with—like this oil contract of yours, John. If you'll forgive plain speaking?" John nodded expressionlessly. "Well, I think you've gone the wrong way about it, old boy. Oh,

I know better than you do how exasperating old
Sulieman can be! Expect Gregor knows it too—we
all do. Not that the Sheikh isn't a decent old thing,
in his way . . .

"Thing is, there's always a young agitator group
in any country these days . . . sorry, Gregor."
Ian grinned. "Don't say you're personally stirring
this pot, but there it is—a nationalist element,
wanting to know what's going on. Might have
been better if Baker revealed day to day progress,
instead of trying to maintain secrecy."

"It wasn't Baker who insisted, but His Highness," John said, leaning forward confidentially.
"No harm in saying so now. We *told* the old man
repeatedly we could prove he was getting the best
possible deal, satisfy the people he was looking
out for their interests. It'd increase his prestige
and flummox the rabble-rousers at the same time.
We said we'd nothing to hide; we even suggested
he work out what suited him, and we'd publish
before final signature to allow time for anyone to
present objections."

John shook his head with a sigh. "He wouldn't
hear of it, Ian. He's advanced in governmental
thinking—but he's still rooted in despotism. He's
going to be *it*, what he says goes, and no Qemani
is going to question the Sheikh's decision. We'd no
choice."

"I suppose not; can't say I think he's wrong, either, with half the country in the desert. Pity,
though. Naturally the agitators consider it's a

challenge. 'Fraid you're in for constant heckling until they know the terms."

"Why?" Gregor inquired. "John wouldn't have the contract, and probably not Baker, either. The copies will be in the Palace, awaiting the end of Ramadan."

Ian raised his eyebrows. "Surely *you* are not so naïve about American business?" He laughed derisively. "My dear Gregor, *who* invented Xerox? All the originals may be with old Sulieman, but there'll be at least a dozen copies—just in case."

"In case of what?" Nita asked innocently.

"In case of a palace explosion."

"I *thought* that number three wife was a mistake," Anna-Venezuela commented indistinctly, swallowing a mouthful of beef with gusto.

Nita and I chorused, "What's wrong with number three wife?"

Anna shrugged. "She's the daughter of Abou ibn-Ferid—the one nobody would marry."

Nita persisted. "Why not?"

"Because she thinks," Anna stated tersely. "She's like that Shakespeare girl Kate. Even for fifty camels, nobody would have her."

"Why did the Sheikh marry her, then? Certainly he doesn't need another fifty camels."

"No, but he does need the friendship of Abou ibn-Ferid," Anna said calmly, "and in the end it was useless, because Abou has learned Sulieman does not sleep with Faria. I wonder how they got that gossip out of the palace?"

"If it comes to that, how did *you?*" Ian asked, suavely.

She was sampling the salad appreciatively. "Mmmm! Delicious! How?" she asked, surprised. "But you know how, Ian—our jobs are the same, after all. Fran, where does the beef come from? Not frozen, surely?"

"I don't know where Baker gets it—I don't manage the kitchen here, you know."

"No, it is Ibrahim's younger brother," she agreed. "I forgot. Gregor, when do you go to the desert?"

I sat with my eyes on my dinner plate, allowing the conversation to wash over me and eating automatically. Abou ibn-Ferid? Azriel's brother, Fatuoma's desert uncle, the Bedouin sheikh in the rear of the rug shop we were not to visit again because it was the headquarters of the nationalists— and whom Ian had accompanied into Qeman the day Nita arrived? It had to be one and the same man. And now Gregor was also to visit that desert camp. I could hear Gregor making light of the trip, but his voice was faintly disconcerted. Oh, bless Anna for opening my ears—and I must, I *would* remember her name, once someone told me what it was.

Why should Gregor visit Abou ibn-Ferid's camp? He was saying it was merely to escort a Russian nomadic group. He looked forward to his first experience of a Bedouin camp.

"First? I thought you went out last year."

"Yes, on Sulieman's royal progress." Gregor shrugged.

"A bit different to be on your own, handling nomads without a common language."

Russian nomads? What a perfect cover for egging Abou to make trouble! All Gregor needed was the contract, and tonight was the perfect opportunity, with the entire foreign colony gathered here. Did I dare phone Ibrahim to be particularly on guard?

And that was another thing—his younger brother was *here?* Was he another local CID man? Where had he been the day Ibrahim came to rescue me from Baker's servants? Was he the one who'd had eye surgery at Djurdel? Ibrahim had said, "Now he sees," but was that simply one degree better than blindness?

We were up to dessert, but back to the burglar, dammit.

Ian said, "I'm only surprised you were disturbed, John. I'd think the first place to look would be in Baker's safe."

"Nonsense!" Nita scoffed. "You're thinking Western. I'm surprised at you, Ian. If the thing is really important, it won't be in a safe at all."

"You would put it in the living room among some magazines, like the Purloined Letter?" Gregor asked, and smiled.

"Oh, that's been overdone, don't you think?" Nita parried lightly. "I've no idea where a man would hide a paper."

"Where would a woman hide it—among her powder puffs?"

A horrible telepathy told me exactly what Nita would reply. There she sat, just out of reach of a nudge from my toe, ready to open her lovely mouth and spill the beans in a heap. Gregor's sleek head was bent forward, his handsome dark eyes still and shrewd despite the lightness of his tone. It seemed *unbearable* to have got this far toward safety, only to be plunged into the maelstrom again. With all my might, I willed Nita to silence, but I'm evidently not forceful enough for ESP.

"Don't be silly," she said with devastating clarity. "Don't you know women always hide things under their underwear, in the second drawer of the bureau?"

I joined in the general laugh, but on top of my inadvertent discovery, I dared not look at John. I sat with my eyes down, until Ian said, "You're uncommonly silent tonight, Fran. What's the matter?"

"I dropped my napkin." Hastily I slid it to the floor, and craned my neck, peering downward. Bob bent to pick it up, and Sheila started one of her complaints about Oriental servants, who never knew which drawer or shelf was which. The conversation slid into safer channels, but as I raised my head, tucking the napkin onto my lap and glancing about brightly, Gregor's dark eyes met mine for a long, speculative instant.

Originally I'd looked forward to this evening, with some first-class entertainment as a change from the usual native groups wailing on those hideous two-stringed fiddles. Now that the moment had arrived, it seemed endless. I made a beeline for the telephone as soon as we finished dinner; Anna-Venezuela beat me to it, and by the tilt of her head, it was going to be a long conversation. I backtracked for Baker's study, only to encounter our own Fouad. (It was standard procedure to borrow servants for a major wingding. Probably half our staff was in the kitchen, loaned by Ibrahim.) Fouad was carrying a tray of coffee cups and liqueur glasses. He bowed and smiled politely, before whisking into the study, which seemed already smoggy from cigars. So *that* was no good.

Pessimistically, I went upstairs as if to the ladies' room and sped past to John's room, but as I'd expected, the extension was shut off. Naturally. Even the one by Mr. Baker's own bed would be immobilized until he pressed a button in the study. I went back to the guest phone, after powdering my nose, and found a chattering line of young mothers, waiting to check on whether baby Jules (or Hans, Inga, Enrico) had burped satisfactorily and was now asleep.

I gave up and went back to the main room, which was now furnished with neat rows of chairs. There was one man in Qeman who owned the folding-chair concession; he had exactly enough for every person in the foreign colony, including wives. If any consulate or embassy increased its staff, Hassim bought the requisite extra chairs. It was always possible to tell if there were house guests at a major party—somebody would be sitting on chairs culled from study or bedrooms.

Well, if I couldn't get through to Ibrahim, at least I could keep Gregor in view. He was flirting with Sheila, under John's nose, which was tilted at an annoyed angle. There was no sign of Nita and Ian. I went forward and brazenly tucked my arm in Gregor's. "Here you are! Sorry to be so long. Let's find seats before everything's taken. John, Sheila—want to sit with us?"

Gregor's arm stiffened involuntarily. I didn't doubt he was surprised at my calm appropriation. Normally, I was happy to let him interfere with John; why should I be hanging on to him tonight? Before he could recover, I'd settled us neatly in the middle of a row. He wouldn't be able to vanish without crawling over other people, who would remember the inconvenience. . . .

Admittedly, he made no effort to leave. After the first wariness, he seemed entirely content to devote himself to me, although there was a glint in his eyes. We flirted along very pleasantly, delicately increasing the tempo until I was nearly as astonished as Gregor. Who ever dreamed a Communist could be so politely risqué! Whether or not he was fooled, if I wanted to play games, he'd join. . . . But so long as I had him under my eye, I could enjoy the program.

It was terrific. Not since the night Montalva

THE DRIFTING SANDS 191

had sung to us had anyone offered such superior entertainment. The audience was as enthusiastic as an army camp for Bob Hope, though not quite so noisy. And there was an added thrill of pride for me in these American stars, willing to leave the comfort of Broadway or Hollywood to go barnstorming around the world in an effort to make people understand our national personality. John felt it too; he was looking *tall*. At the back of the room, most of the guests were standing for a better view. Glancing around, I could see Nita and Ian poised on adjoining chairs, his arm about her for security, his head bent to hers, laughing intimately. By her expression, Sheila had seen them also.

There were endless encores—our stars were bubbling, working overtime in singing for their suppers. At last, Baker called a halt, or I think they'd have gone on all night, exhausting themselves with generosity. It was nearly midnight, and I felt limp with relief—but the evening wasn't over, after all!

There was the usual milling about, while Hassim's men swiftly folded and removed the chairs. The entertainers were mingling graciously. I'd once met a couple of them, which gave me a chance to drag Gregor along for handshaking and praise. He came so willingly that I felt uneasy . . .

I was even more uneasy to observe Sir Percival and his peers jovially retreating to the bridge tables! What the hell were they hanging around for? Midnight was always tacitly understood to be the end of an evening, the moment for the ranking diplomat to leave and release everyone else. Apparently tonight Old Perce meant to whoop it up. They were drawing for partners, settling down cozily, being furnished with drinks. Now it was impossible for anyone to leave until the final rubber, meaning I must still keep an eye on Gregor—unless I could reach John.

I couldn't. He was already caught to partner Mevrouw Vandam, the Dutch Ambassador's wife (resplendent in cocoa-brown silk with a necklace of Javanese yellow sapphires), against Sir Percival, who was happily greeting Anna-Venezuela to make the fourth. "What *is* Anna's last name?" I asked Gregor desperately. "I feel such a fool, but I can never remember these complicated Latin names."

"Her name is Salvador, and probably the reason you cannot remember is because it is *not* complicated," Gregor remarked. "Shall we dance, Fran?"

"Oh, yes, let's do." The chairs were gone, the orchestra was beginning in the long room, and already the floor was filling. Far at the other end I could see the portable bar trundled into place and instantly surrounded by thirsty guests. Bob stepped in pro tem, until the bar servant should arrive. Ian and Nita were drifting about gracefully, just short of cheek-to-cheek. Sheila was dancing with one of the Danes, and Gregor steered me slowly toward the bar.

"You seem unusually tired tonight, Fran—or is there something on your mind?"

"No; only tired. I wish this whole silly mess were over."

"Don't worry; it will be. Instead of dancing, would you prefer a drink in the garden?"

"Yes, if you don't mind."

It was the wrong decision. Gregor swept me to a stand before the bar, where Bob fixed our drinks, saying, "Don't know where the drink boy is. Baker asked if I'd stand in till he shows."

"He'll never show up, if you're willing to do his job," Gregor remarked, picking up our glasses. "You're stuck to closing, Penniston."

"Oh, I don't mind." Bob winked. "Saves my feet. . . ."

We went out to the garden. Gregor settled me in a group of Mexicans mixed with a Lebanese girl and assorted Central Americans—the younger set, in fact, and all speaking Spanish, although they politely changed to English for my benefit. Gregor stood behind my chair, joining in the conversation casually but looking in to the dance floor. When the music changed to a seductive Latin rhythm, he drained his glass and bent to my ear. "You will forgive me if I leave you with Manuel?" he murmured. "John is—incommunicado, after all, and someone must rescue Sheila from that Danish lout—she detests him."

It was the neatest brush-off of the season. The group was disposing itself into couples; Manuel was gallantly reaching for my hand . . . I had no choice but to watch Gregor smilingly bow himself away to Sheila, who was sitting at the bar. She brightened slightly when Gregor cut away the Dane. Looking over Manuel's shoulder, I thought Frans was equally relieved to be rid of Sheila. He was on his feet instantly, waving Gregor into his stool and turning to survey the dance floor, literally rubbing his hands together before heading toward a pretty Norwegian secretary.

Sheila took most of the dance to finish her drink, with both Gregor and Bob laughing and leaning toward her confidentially, but finally she was on the floor in Gregor's arms. Manuel and I came alongside, and Gregor spared a smile for me, but he was whispering into Sheila's ear. Whatever he said must have been right, for she tittered and burrowed against his shoulder. Moving around the floor, I could see John still at the bridge table, looking expressionless—meaning Old Perce was being more intransigent than usual. Anna-Venezuela (I *must* remember Salvador!) was lighting a cigarette, glancing out to the dance floor while Sir Percival began the play. She caught my eye and waved, smiling—but having been in her place, I knew it was simply that she couldn't bear to watch the shambles occurring on the table.

Nita and Ian were still drifting about dreamily, until they reached the bar end, where Ian got a couple of drinks and took her out to the garden. After that, I was forced to concentrate on my footwork, since Manuel was becoming fancy, so the music ended before I realized Gregor was gone.

I had no idea how or when, but Sheila was

parked alone on a barstool, and there was no sign
of her partner. Clever Gregor—how easily he'd got
rid of my surveillance, damn him! The mere fact
that he'd ditched me was proof I was on the right
track. He'd played along until it suited him, but
he hadn't been fooled—and now he knew exactly
where to look—in a bureau drawer. He wouldn't
find the contract in my room or Nita's; he'd look
in every chest—and long before this hellish party
ended, he'd have found the thing.

All that he wouldn't find, please God, was Elvig's films—because he didn't know they existed.
Once he had the contract, surely he wouldn't
bother prising off the padlock—would he?

If Fouad was here, so would be all the rest of
our staff, leaving only Ibrahim. I excused myself
to Manuel and hastily went out to the guest
phone. It was in use.

Gregor Semirov sat in the booth, cuddling the
phone to his ear, a fatuous smile on his face. He
was the epitome of a man talking to his mistress
cajoling, explaining a broken rendezvous. Half-
turned from the hall, he hadn't seen me. He was
speaking Arabic. The accents were faint through
the door, but there was no question of the timbre.

His was not The Voice.

9

I retreated to the ladies' room, feeling thoroughly confused. I'd been *certain*—but if it were not Gregor, who was it?

At least he was still here, instead of rifling my bureau drawers . . . or was the phone call another cleverness? No; he'd no reason to think I'd see him in the booth, and if he were giving instructions to a subordinate, he'd have kept an eye out for anyone approaching in the hall. I might not understand Arabic, but any number of other guests did.

Tangentially, my mind said, "He's got a native girl? Wonder if Berthe Drouet knows *that!*" I thought perhaps I'd ask her next week . . . and went downstairs again. I couldn't resist a peek at the phone booth. Gregor was still in it. His mistress was either difficult to placate or a very fascinating conversationalist. I still wasn't easy of mind, but a quick tour of bridge and dance rooms showed no one obviously absent. John's table was pivoting; it was now men against women, Sir Percival his partner. When I wandered by, he was looking rather taller than usual and somewhat in favor of resigning his seat to me, but Old Perce wouldn't hear of it.

"You can go dance at the end of this rubber," he stated. "Won't be long now—but I won't have your wife. She nearly gave me a heart attack the other night. Erratic, that's what she is. No biddin' sense whatever—and then she makes it because she doesn't know how to play. Confusin' gel, young man—too confusin' for me. Go away, Fran; you'll put me off m'game."

I suppressed the query "What game?" and left John to his fate. He might as well be playing bridge as dancing with Sheila. Either way, we couldn't leave until Sir Percival was satiated, and I had enough on my mind already. I went back to the dance floor and had a partner at once—there were always enough unmarried youngsters to go around. At a glance, the status was still quo but looking more hopeful. Several of the bridge tables were through, adding to the crowd until Sir Percival finished. Madame Drouet was toddling about with Frans, and Mr. Iandouros was piloting his wife in stately circles. Mr. Baker was on the floor, and Henri had "emerged" to talk with Mrs. Tomyienkov. Bob was still tending bar, and Sheila . . .

Looking over my partner's shoulder, I couldn't understand why Sheila was alone at the bar—until I glimpsed Bob's bland face. Every time she turned her head, Bob refilled her glass. Sheila was rapidly growing high, then tight, and finally stoned. Her voice was strident, raised over the music but too slurred for interpretation. She teetered on the stool, bracing herself on the bar and leaning forward to clutch Bob's hand. He didn't seem to be saying much, but I knew he wasn't missing a word of her maudlin confidences. What I couldn't fathom was why he'd deliberately made her drunk. Could he be trying, on his own, to break her from John? It wouldn't work—I felt positive of that.

John has an aphorism: You see many pretty women drunk; you will never see a pretty drunk woman. But Sheila did not habitually drink too much. She was not a lush, attested by the ease with which only a few drinks were affecting her. If anything, John would be furious at Bob for creating disgrace for the woman he loved—if he did love her, and perhaps he did, no matter what Berthe Drouet thought. He'd certainly wanted to get away from Sir Percival. Old Perce wasn't fooled, although he tactfully hadn't specified John's dance partner by name. Well, he wouldn't, of course, with John's wife standing there. . . .

It still wouldn't work, even if Sheila fell off that stool, which she showed every likelihood of doing. John would only pick her up and consider one isolated incident forgivable. If anything, he'd be more tender and compassionate because it wasn't her fault.

As luck would have it, the music ended exactly as I was near the bar. I looked the other way, but before I could get my partner to take me to the garden, Sheila saw me. "You!" she said. "You're at the bottom of this. You think I don't know, but I do, too right I do."

"Nonsense, Sheila," Bob said easily. "Fran wouldn't do anything to hurt you."

"Not much she wouldn't!" Sheila spat. "Thinks she can get round Ian by inviting me and his children to Lebanon, huh? An' after we got there, she'd conveniently be called back." She laughed mirthlessly. "Outsmarted herself this time. You don't know y'r precious Ian as well 's I do."

I looked at her wavering body and glassy eyes and thought, Oh, no! It only needed this, for the explosion to be tonight of all nights. Madame Drouet had said it would not be pretty, and it wasn't, but why did it have to be so ill-timed? "Please, Sheila, I don't know what you're talking about," I placated, trying to move away. But she was off the barstool with drunken speed, lurching forward to grasp my arm violently. "You don't?" she said thickly. "Then I'll tell you, what've I got to lose? Ian'll never look at you or any woman, 'less she has money. Y'think your frien's face matt'rs? She could be a hundred years old an' ugly as sin . . . wouldn' matter to Ian." She made a disdainful gesture with her hand, nearly overbalanced, and saved herself by catching the barstool. Bob made an infinitesimal gesture, and the orchestra started up again.

"You," he said to my partner, "go away, will you? Get someone else, and dance at this end, so nobody sees? Until we get her on her feet and out."

"*Sí; sí, ciertamente,*" the kid said hurriedly, backing away.

"Dammit, *now* what?" I said to Bob, trying to loosen Sheila's painful grasp on my wrist. "She's drunk as a skunk; you made her this way—you cope."

He came out from behind the bar, but before he could pry her loose from me, there was a small break in the crowd of dancers, giving all of us a clear view of Nita. She was coming into the room from the farther garden door, and if ever a girl looked bemused by a recent, very thorough kissing, it was she. Ian was instantly behind her, murmuring into her ear. Beside me Sheila drew a long sobbing breath, while Nita turned and swayed into Ian's arms like a flame seeking a steady draft to burn straight.

"He won't get away with it," Sheila muttered. "Won' stan' for it."

"Shhh. You're quite wrong. Come upstairs and lie down for a minute." Now it was *happening,* I didn't want it to happen. I had no choice, even with Bob shielding us from the dancers, who were already casting curious glances our way.

"Go along with Fran, Sheila. I'll get Ian, tell him you're not feeling well." Bob's voice was solicitous, but whose fault was it Sheila was stoned? Whatever he'd been trying to do, it was going to backfire on me, I thought furiously, trying to tug her away to the hall before the dancing stream brought Ian and Nita into sight.

"Come along, sweetie; I'll help you. Come on, just a step at a time, *that's* the way, lean on me, come on. . . ." It was useless—she could scarcely stand, let alone move. I'd got her a bare two yards toward the door, when she stopped dead and violently thrust me away.

"*No;* don' want you. I know y'r game, and his too." Sheila pulled herself erect with determination and stared at the dancing circle that was bringing Ian and Nita closer and closer.

"Bob!" I said, pleadingly, but before he could move in front of Sheila, she'd seen them and taken a few steps toward Ian.

"This is the chance you've been waiting for, isn't it?" she hissed at him, her voice low and venomous. "Well, you can't have it without me! I've dragged aroun' in poverty and slums with you for ten years 'n' done y'r dirty work for you—you'll not push *me* aside when you get a chance for money 'n' a soft life."

"Shut up!" he said roughly. "You're drunk." He tried to steer Nita away, but she stood firm, her face white but determined.

"What sort of dirty work do you mean?"

Ian's eyes glazed. "Sheila!" he said warningly, but she ignored him.

"I mean all these stories of unhappiness and brutality, and flirting with someone who might be useful. I'm unhappy—too right I am—but I'm sick of trying to lure some man into giving Ian a better break." Sheila's eyes grew dim with self-pity. "Oh, you'd have to do it too, no matter how much money you had! Holding hands in a garden, kissing men you don't even like . . ."

Ian made a quick movement; Nita was quicker still. "Do you usually slap your wife in public?" she asked with icy clarity, striking his arm down.

"Let him strike me!" Sheila said wildly. "I might as well be dead as the way I am. Except he'd like to be a widower, so he could marry a rich woman. Poor Ian," she hiccuped with alcoholic laughter, "always trying to strike it rich, always jus' missing—and it's always *my* fault, 'cause I can't make an impression on the right person—or maybe it's jus' because I exist at all, so *he* can' make an impression on right person."

She swayed backward a few steps, pointing a finger at him, her laughter rising in maudlin hysteria. "He's a dis'pointed gigolo, that's what he is. Never made a deal yet, for all the chances he's had—but he keeps right on trying." She closed her eyes, moaning pitifully, and lurched so far to the right that I thought she'd overbalance and collapse on the floor. Instinctively I grabbed her hand, while Bob propped her from the other side. Together, we made a sort of protective screen, but it wasn't enough to disguise the situation completely. The musicians were doing their best, playing louder and not breaking for the usual change of rhythm. I could see the leader keeping a shrewd eye on us; he'd be well used to drunks, and undoubtedly he'd keep the music going until we'd disposed of Sheila—which wasn't going to be easy, short of forcibly carrying her out of the place.

She was muttering over and over, "Won't have it, won't let him . . ." Most of the guests tactfully continued dancing; a few nearby couples stopped hesitantly, wondering if they should offer help. Suddenly Sheila's voice soared raucously, "*Sick* of it, sick to *death* of him . . . but he keeps right on tryin' to fin' the gold key that'll open all doors. *Wha'* doors?" she asked scornfully. "Can't do it himself, wants *out*, 'n settle f'r bankroll."

Swiftly, Ian thrust past Nita and laid hold of his wife. "God! Are you out of your mind, Sheila?" he asked hoarsely. "Accusing me like this, in public . . . you *know* it's not true; you *promised* . . . Your insane jealousy will get me bounced from the only job I know, if you keep on. Please, sweetheart, shhhh." With unexpected tenderness, he held her shuddering body against him, stroking her hair, murmuring gently, while she buried her face against his shoulder with a sob and clung to him.

"Jealous, tha's it," she wailed abjectly. "Oh, Ian, so sorry. . . . forgive, forgive please? Can't bear . . . mus'nt lose you . . . *please?*"

"Shhhh. It's all right, darling. Shhhh." Whitefaced, he raised his head, looking at the ring of silent, shocked guests. "I must beg you to excuse my wife," he said, with pure British formality. "She is—unwell from the heat, and inclined to fancy difficulties where none exist. Come, sweetheart." His head high, he quietly guided her stumbling feet through the guests toward the hall.

Bob moved forward quickly, drawing Nita away to the garden. The dancers resumed, in a subdued buzz of gossip. I stood shakily, staring after the Haysraths and feeling the most complete heel. How could I have been so thoughtless, so self-centered as to lay the powder train that might cost Ian his job? Granted, Bob had lit the fuse by making Sheila drunk, but Ian had only verified what I suspected—he did care for his wife. The dignity with which he'd calmed her and taken her away was impressive. Worst of all, it was all for nothing. John was still in the bridge room, his back to the hall. He'd seen and heard no hint of the explosion.

Sheila's bag still lay on the edge of the bar. Instinctively, I picked it up and ran after them, but just as I reached the hall door, their car had been brought from the parking space. Fouad was evidently doubling in brass. He slid out of the driver's seat and, in response to a few words from Ian, came quickly forward to assist Sheila's wavering form down the front path and into the car seat. Ian was putting a good face on the situation, tossing a couple of coins to Fouad with an easy smile before sliding behind the wheel. I could see him solicitously making Sheila comfortable, with some comment that drew a smile from Fouad. Then the Haysraths were gone.

But I still had her purse, and her wrap must still be upstairs; they hadn't waited for a servant to get it—not that it mattered. Nobody could possibly get a cold in Qeman, except for ebullient air-conditioning. I leaned against the door jamb, and frankly I felt sick with myself.

"*Alors, ne t'en blâme pas, Françoise; ce fut inevitable.*" Berthe Drouet smiled at me, patting my hand. I could see her dance partner loitering tactfully out of earshot.

"She left her purse," I said, foolishly, feeling tears in my eyes. "Oh, I *wish* I hadn't . . ."

"Go upstairs and put with 'er wrap, chérie, and do *not* blame yourself," she repeated firmly. "Put it out of your mind."

"How can I, when it may have cost Ian his post?"

"*Quant à ça*; that too was inevitable," she said cryptically. "No tears. You have perhaps done better than you know. Put the bag with her wrap, wipe your eyes, powder your nose, and come back until it is ended. *Dépêche-toi.*" She gave me a little push and went back to her partner, smiling at me as they moved away and were lost in the crowd of dancers.

The floor was full. It was as though, with Ian's departure, the social waters had closed over his head. He and Sheila had never existed, and the incident had never happened. Could it be so easily erased? I knew I would never forget it, never cease to be remorseful, no matter what madame Drouet said.

Dully, I noted Bob dancing with Nita, madame Iandouros talking with monsieur Drouet, while her husband was bouncing about with the wife of a Spanish attaché in a Greek version of the samba. Looking the other way, I could see bridge tables beginning to empty, people adding up, settling up, rising to stretch cramped muscles. The decorative wall clock said one-thirty, but John was still caught. Worse yet, Mr. Baker was jovially making up a new foursome of people bored with dancing . . . meaning that Sir Percival would demand another rubber. The only way to get him away from a bridge table was to clear out the room and let him discover he was preventing everyone else from leaving.

Wearily, I turned to the stairs, holding Sheila's shoddy white satin bag. Halfway up the stairs I stopped, feeling a shiver of pure terror working up my spine. The telephone booth was still softly lit— it was empty.

Where was Gregor Semirov?

I sped back to the dance floor and peered about, but there was no sign of him. I told myself he could be in the garden or have gone to the hoo-ha, and I didn't believe it. Had he ducked out for an assignation with his mistress, chancing his absence wouldn't be noticed in the general exodus when this horrible party ended? Mrs. Tomyienkov was placidly discussing housekeeping problems with the wife of the Turkish ambassador, while Tomyienkov procured tots of vodka at the bar, where a servant had finally shown up. He came back, carefully balancing the three glasses, and joined his wife, sitting down contentedly and rais-

ing his glass with a smile for the two women.
Madame Beyda said something that widened his
smile to a chuckle and drew a positive snort from
Mrs. Tomyienkov. Did they know Gregor's where-
abouts?

The Russian Ambassador was the picture of en-
joyment. As he tossed off his drink, he saw me
poised on the doorway. Instantly, he was beckoning, indicating a chair beside them. "Mrs. Kennett, you are not dancing? Join us until your husband is finished."

"Oh, no, thank you so much, Your Excellency—I
was only looking for Mr. Semirov, to tell him I
was going upstairs for a moment."

"Gregor?" Tomyienkov looked about vaguely.
"He is somewhere about. I do not see him, but
please to sit with us. Let me get you a drink?"

"Thank you, no. . . ." But the Russian Ambassador was on his feet, presenting a chair, smiling
politely.

His wife was equally smiling, patting the seat
of the chair. "Come, sit with us, Mrs. Kennett, until Gregor returns."

I shook my head, "I only wanted to say I was
going to powder my nose. If you see him, say I'll
be back in a minute?"

"Of course; of course."

But I hadn't missed the sudden sharpness in Tomyienkov's eyes when I mentioned his attaché or
the tiny flicker of a glance from him to his wife. It
might mean nothing more than surprise that *I* was
searching for Gregor, when he was considered

more or less Sheila's property—or it might mean that he knew quite well where Gregor was and was disconcerted to have the absence remarked.

The phone booth was still lit. I slid inside and rang our house. There was no answer.

But Ibrahim must be there. Even if he'd lent some of our servants for the evening—even if he'd allowed the others a night off for celebration of the end of Ramadan—I couldn't picture Ibrahim leaving the place deserted. . . . Had I made a mistake in the dialing, because of nerves? I hung up and tried again, concentrating on each number. I let it ring interminably—in case he were asleep . . . or having to come in from the garden . . . or through the courtyard and kitchen. . . . There was still no answer.

I replaced the phone finally and gripped the wooden shelf, trying to think what best to do. On top of the scene with Sheila, any insistence on breaking up the bridge game for John to take me home would only be additional sensation, piling Ossa on Pelion. Even if I could get hold of Bob, there was too much to explain, too many whys and wherefores—but pulling myself out of the booth, I was more and more convinced with every step that unless someone got back to our house on the double, someone else was going to find the contract—might even now be searching. . . .

Setting Sheila's bag in the pocket of her sham-ermine evening stole, and unconsciously noting how pitifully worn the edges were, I told myself it was only in books that all Russians are automatically spies. It was useless. I couldn't rid myself of the absolute certainty that Gregor was the mastermind, that Tomyienkov knew it, and that that was why he'd been so anxious for me to join them. If I didn't get the hell out of the cloakroom in a hurry, Mrs. Tomyienkov would be sent to check up. . . .

Quietly, I slid my wrap from its hanger, not waking the maid, who was sound asleep in her chair, and got the hell out, turning the other way from the cloakroom and not sure exactly what I meant to do. Shadows on the wall, footsteps on the carpeted stairs . . . Instinctively I faded back to the curve of the hall where Ibrahim had found me, and cautiously I squatted down and peeked around the corner. Mrs. Tomyienkov and madame Beyda were going into the cloakroom.

That did it.

It was all I needed to reinforce my female illogic. Thanks to Ibrahim, now I knew which door led to the servants' stairs, but could I get away without being seen? Did it matter if I were seen? Pulling open the door, I listened and heard only a few voices below, the slam of a refrigerator door, then silence. Slipping off my shoes, I went softly down to the rear hall, lurking in the shadows to orient myself. The pantry and kitchen were spotless, dishes washed and put away, all servants gone. Ahead of me was the garden door, standing open for whatever breath of air it would bring. In the kitchen to my right was only one yawning servant, on duty to provide more ice or hot coffee. He was turned away from me, occupied with a sink full of dirty glasses . . . but as he rinsed and set them to dry, he turned to the left. Sleepy as he was, he'd notice any flash of movement from the stairs. . . .

Luck was with me. The service door swung open, someone gave a sharp command in Arabic, and the man went with a grunt to open the huge refrigerator. As the door swung out at right angles, screening off the rear hall, I made the garden door in three long steps. Half a dozen trash cans flanked the exit. I picked my way cautiously out to the alley, where the car boys were squatting at the curb waiting for the party to end. They were absorbed in some Arab gambling game, and the onlookers stood with their backs to me, bending over the players. I went the other way, into the shadows of the alley behind the Russian Embassy, going slowly from one patch of darkness to another. There was no sign of life in their garage or servants' quarters.

Finally I'd gained the street and turned toward our house. It must have been two in the morning by now, and Qeman seemed blamelessly asleep. The revels for the end of Ramadan would long since have withdrawn to the privacy of back rooms in native homes. I was still carrying my shoes. I'd originally taken them off to prevent any sound of heels on cobblestones, but now I realized I'd make better speed in stockinged feet, and never mind if the stockings snagged. Faintly, from the center of the town, I could hear pipes and drums, but this was the foreign colony, and despite the dim-lit streets, I never thought of being afraid.

I trotted along at a moderate pace, passing one after another of the embassies, meeting no one and hearing no sound, until I reached our own corner. There, I slowed and reconnoitered again. I was perfectly convinced in my own mind that Gregor was at the bottom of all the spying and burgling, that he was either already in our house or due momentarily. I hadn't stopped to consider what he was likely to do if I caught him; I thought only of getting home, getting the contract out of that bureau drawer, and putting it—where?

Under my mattress! . . .

What a *good* idea, I applaused myself. Why hadn't I thought of it before? Anyway, it'd be perfect, until John got home. I made a plan—I'd put the contract under the mattress, undress, and go to bed on top of the thing.

That is, if Gregor hadn't beaten me to it—but in that case, I'd telephone for John at once, which would lead to immediate and very embarrassing questions, because Gregor and the Tomyienkovs wouldn't expect the loss to be discovered so quickly.

Peering around the corner, I sensed rather than saw a breath of motion at the farther end of the street—white-robed figures. Were they merely servants from one of the houses beyond ours, or were they thieves? In any Oriental country, half the populace lives by stealing from the other half, or so the saying goes. My white dress was all too noticeable, but fortunately the wrap was dark. I hiked up the long skirts and wrapped the scarf above my head to cover as much as possible of my face . . . and still the figures at the other corner hadn't moved. I decided they must be servants; thieves wouldn't loiter like that, and if they were connected with Gregor, there'd be a lookout at this corner too.

One step at a time, holding my skirts firmly concealed under the evening coat, I sidled along the wall to our driveway and ducked inside. I felt fairly certain I hadn't been noticed, but my heart was pounding, and I was shaking with nerves. For a moment, I leaned against the palm tree Selim hated because it was twelve inches too close to the drive, making it difficult to turn the car with the pezazz so dear to his heart, but even as my breathing steadied, I was conscious of something . . . something not as usual.

The lamp that always lit the front door until we returned at night was turned out.

I slithered around the palm tree and stood motionless, studying the house, but nowhere could I see a hint of movement or lights, other than the lower-hall chandelier. Perhaps the outer bulb had simply burned out and couldn't be replaced until the boy in charge of light bulbs had returned? I wasn't convinced. Where was Ibrahim? It was unlike him to be unaware of a footstep, however quiet, in the drive. I backtracked soundlessly and felt my way around the shrubbery that screened off the patio. There was still no sign of life anywhere. Very carefully, I went forward, skirting the lounge chairs and tables that were only dark shapes looming in my path, and finally I'd reached the long glass door to the lounge. It was open a half inch, so Ibrahim had to be on the premises—he or one of the servants.

That was it, I thought with relief—Fatuoma and Zoe were here. I'd deliberately not told Fatuoma not to wait up, as extra protection for the darkroom. And knowing she was here, Ibrahim must have taken time off—although I'd have thought he'd be back by now. Anyway, I felt more confident about easing open the door; someone was within earshot of a healthy scream, if required.

Still, I should give Fatuoma no reason to wonder why madam was rooting in the storage chest at two in the morning. I dropped my shoes on a couch and hastened across to the hall. The chandelier was dimmed to lowest power but gave enough light to see by. I'd reached the upper hall, when I thought I heard a noise. What was it, and where? I froze to the newel post, listening . . . hearing nothing but my own pounding temples.

Not Fatuoma—I could see into my bedroom; there was no small shape curled up in the usual spot on the floor, her head resting on hands holding the bottom bedpost. Anyway, she always left a night light burning when she waited for me. There was no repetition of the sound. Had I imagined it?

The dead silence was spooky; it was getting to me. For the first time I *realized* this was no game, no library book with safety on the next page. I had never been more scared in my life. For a plugged nickel I'd have turned tail and run—but I'd come to make certain the contract was safe. I was either ahead of, or behind, Gregor. The only danger was coming face to face with him, but if he were *here,* surely I'd have seen some moving glimmer of light. I might be flattering myself, but I doubted that any interloper could have heard my approach before I sensed his presence.

Finally, the last thing wanted was another murder. In fact, it might be better for me boldly to turn on all the lights. That would disconcert a prowler, whether Gregor or an agent. I'd wake the servants, explain my return as a sudden migraine headache, and go to bed, with Fatuoma bringing aspirin and water.

But first, I must get the contract, if it was there. I gritted my teeth and went down the hall to the storage chest in our extra guest room. There were lighter squares, where windows gave onto the upper gallery outside, but the room was as silent and empty as the rest of the house. There was a tiny terrifying squeak as I pulled out the bottom drawer, but beneath the woollies I could feel paper.

Despite my relief, I felt uncommonly foolish. I sat on the floor and told myself severely, "You've been reading too many thrillers, my girl!" I could almost have laughed—except . . . *now* what? I'd scared myself half to death getting back here to preserve the contract . . . there were still Ross Elvig's films, for which, I had no doubt, he'd been killed . . . and we still had a spy.

Whether or not my expression had given away the secret at dinner, Nita's light words would have suggested a new point of departure. And whether or not Gregor was the spy, I was certain he'd added two and two to make five. Yet why hadn't he got it? He'd certainly used the Haysrath explosion to cover his disappearance, and he'd had a good twenty-minute head start. Where was he? Cuddling in the hay with his girlfriend? The whole situation reversed in my mind. Tomyienkov's eagerness to detain me and his attempt to suppress questions about his attaché were only cover-ups for a perfectly normal relationship of which he was undoubtedly quite aware. Mrs. Tomyienkov and madame Beyda had gone to the cloakroom because they had to, not because they were looking for me.

And I had gone off half-cocked, rushing home to protect something that was in no danger! Gregor might have whispered his conclusion to his boss, but that would have been *finito*. No Russian is a blabbermouth; it's hard to get them to give you so much as the current weather report when it's snowing outside. Ergo, nobody but our own table had heard Nita—and all were blamelessly disposed. Bob and Nita were dancing, but they were outside it all, in any case. John and Anna-Venezuela (Salvador) were playing bridge, and the Haysraths were home, where he was presumably putting her to bed.

What a total idiot I'd been. Nobody knew anything; nobody was going to try a second search. Sadly, I admitted to myself that I was a big baby. I should have stayed in Toledo instead of prancing around Qeman and stirring the pot till it boiled over. Face it, I was never meant for intrigue or diplomacy. All I could hope was to save my red face, go to bed, and trust that John would never suspect my folly.

I was perfectly calm, back to normal, and about to close the drawer, when I heard soft footsteps on the outer gallery. Ibrahim, of course, making rounds. In a few seconds, sure enough, a tall figure in Arab robes appeared in the farther window. "Ibrahim?" I said hastily, as a pencil-torch light flashed into the room, moving slowly toward me. "Don't be alarmed; it's only me—I was just hunting for my headache medicine."

There was a slight grunt of surprise, and the beam swung to catch me, blinding me to the person behind it. For a split second the torch wavered, and terror engulfed me. "Ibrahim?" I asked quaveringly. "Is that you?"

I knew it wasn't. . . .

"No, my dear Fran, it is not Ibrahim," said Ian Haysrath, "nor are you looking for migraine pills." He set one long leg, evening-trousered beneath the white robes, over the window sill and stepped into the room.

"You!" I said in the best tradition of stupidity.

"I, myself, and me, dear Fran," he agreed, and in the backlight of his torch, I could see a very unpleasant little gun in his right hand, pointing directly at me. "I confess I hadn't anticipated a personal guide to the exact spot, but since you're here, it'd save time if you'd just hand me the contract."

Well, I hadn't the faintest idea what I was going to say until I'd said it. "The hell I will. And stop waving that gun around. You don't frighten me, Ian Haysrath, and if it goes off, you'll be in a worse spot than ever," I told him crossly.

He snorted. "I couldn't be in a worse spot, *due to you*, my poppet."

"Okay, I'm sorry. I never meant a blast-off, Ian—truly I didn't. So if you'll get the hell out of here, I'll forget I ever saw you."

"A generous offer, but I'll take the contract with me."

"Oh, *quit* being dramatic, will you? I told you before, not on your life." I was unable to take him seriously. I was beginning to scramble to my feet, when his voice stopped me.

"Not my life, Francesca *mia*—yours."

He might have been fairly sober at the party, but now he was the better, or worse, for whatever he'd downed while he was putting Sheila to bed. With sudden horror, I realized that Ian had killed Ross. And now that I'd identified him, how could he avoid killing me, too? It must have shown in my face, because he laughed recklessly. "Exactly! But you're safe enough if I have that paper—not that it wouldn't be a pleasure to dispose of you, my dear. After the damned mess you cooked up for me tonight, what have I got to lose?" His voice was vicious. "Doesn't matter now, luckily. I'll have enough money from Abou ibn-Ferid to be able to shake the diplomatic dust out of my hair." He took a few steps toward me, holding out his hand imperiously. "Hurry up; give."

My hand moved convulsively in the drawer, felt solidity, and closed around the collapsible travelling umbrella. Slowly I turned, pulling out the contract with my left hand and raising myself to sprinting position. Ian was standing directly beside me, the gun held steady but the torch wavering in two fingers, leaving three to grasp the paper. He hadn't seen my makeshift weapon; it was worth a try . . .

Whirling, I came upright and brought the umbrella crashing down on his gun hand almost simultaneously. The gun went off with a hideous noise, and the bullet buried itself in the floor. He grunted in pain, but before he could aim, I'd beaten his knuckles again, and I heard the gun dropping from his fingers. Then I pushed him violently away from me and raced for the door. He was after me at once. I'd gained no more than a few seconds, and my only advantage was knowing the house better than he did in the dark.

Tumbling wildly down the stairs, I sought desperately in my mind for somewhere to ditch the contract temporarily. Where *was* everyone? Why did no one come to investigate that gunshot? I tugged the hall bellpull as I ran past to John's study. There was just time to slam the door and turn the key in Ian's face. He wouldn't be put off, naturally. I could hear him dashing on along the hall; he'd go out and around through the garden. I slid the contract flat on the floor under a corner of the rug and ran for the long windows, but there were too many of them. Why were they unfastened in the first place? I managed to bolt two, but Ian faced me through the third, and his pressure forced me away. I abandoned the windows and darted to the study bellpull.

Ian's hand spun me around. "You interfering bitch! By God, I *should've* got rid of you upstairs." Seizing my wrist in an iron grip, he twisted until I screamed with pain. "Go on, scream! The servants have been taken care of. Where are the papers, damn you?"

Maddened by pain, I went berserk, clawing his face until my fingernails broke, drawing blood. I couldn't kick, for I was still in stockinged feet. I tried getting a knee to his groin, but the Arab robes over his evening trousers made that impossible. All the time, he was forcing me slowly sideways, off balance . . . but in the process he had to bend over, and finally I bit his ear.

I really *bit* it too—I could taste blood, but I hadn't time for nausea. He yelled with pain and instinctively relaxed the wrist grip, trying to free himself. I was still hanging on to him like a bulldog, and eventually we'd both had enough of it. He let go of my wrist, to use both hands in fighting me off—and I let go of his ear with a simultaneous push that sent him staggering back against John's desk.

He was like a wild man. Cursing and brushing blood from his scratches, he leaped at me; I slid around the desk and he caught only the back drapery of my dress. It tore free with a sharp ripping sound, and as he lunged again, I threw John's heavy glass ashtray at him. It whizzed past his shoulder and crashed through one of the garden windows. The sound reverberated through the still night air—but he'd said the servants were taken care of. I no longer expected anyone to come to my rescue, and the instant he could get his hands on me, I'd be done for. I knew that. I was no longer protecting John's contract—now I was fighting for my life.

Ian was no longer after the contract, either. If he hadn't dropped the gun, abandoned it in favor of seeing where I went with the papers, I'd be a dead duck already. We were both panting from exertion, bathed in blood, sweat, and (in my case) tears. We were wasting no energy on speech but dodging back and forth silently. My mind was astonishingly clear. Ian had lost the gun, but he'd still have a knife, like the one he'd used on Ross Elvig. He hadn't produced it yet, keeping his hands free to catch me, but once he'd got me, the knife would appear. Well, I didn't need two free hands—I wasn't trying to catch him. Automatically, I grasped John's letter opener. It was not much of a weapon, but it was better than nothing.

Never laugh again at jokes about men chasing women around a bed! If you've ever been chased by a man grimly determined to kill you, it's much too horrifying, even in retrospect. Ian and I feinted this way and that for what seemed a geologic eon, and try as I would, I couldn't get him away from his strategic position between me and the one open window. Once, he made a frontal attack across the desk and captured my hand, but dull as it was, the paper knife served to numb his fingers and set me free. The room was a shambles of overturned chairs, broken glass, torn scraps of my dress.

Oh, that ill-fated dress! I'd worn it the night of Ross's murder—I'd worn it tonight, which might well end in my own murder. It was hanging in shreds over one shoulder, flapping across the brassiere beneath, half the skirt was ripped away . . . I'd stuff it in the incinerator tomorrow morning, if I were alive or had the strength—which seemed unlikely.

I was no match for the energy of Ian Haysrath's body. I could feel myself flagging . . . it was only a question of time. Only the instinctive will to live kept me going. I'd never known I *had* this much energy, even if it was a losing battle, and finally there was the blessed sound of a racing motor stopping outside. Doors slammed; then I heard voices and running footsteps. . . .

With my last remaining strength, I screamed, "JOHN—*in the study!*"

I'd relaxed my guard to yell. Ian leapt at me

like a maniac. "Bloody *bitch!*" he shouted. He threw off my last feeble attempt to use the paper knife and gave me what I later learned was a commando punch. It should have killed me, except that I was so exhausted I was already dropping to the floor, and his angle was off. As it was, I simply got a hit on the head and went out like a light.

10

I came to, lying on a couch in the lounge, with Nita sobbing softly beside me and a figure in Arab robes standing over us. Involuntarily I moaned in remembered terror and twisted aside. "Ian?"

"Shhh. No, Mrs. Kennett. It is Doctor Amahl; you are quite safe." A second white-robed figure stepped forward.

"Ibrahim?"

"Yes, madam."

I closed my eyes wearily. "Where the hell were you?"

"Drugged in the servants' quarters. Miss Janus, reassure her, please."

"Yes. It's all over, darling, all safe. Lie still and rest."

"If you say so."

I must have gone to sleep instantly, holding Nita's hand. The next time I awoke, I was in my own bed. It was broad daylight beyond the tilted blinds, and the room was crammed with people. Nita was asleep, cuddled in Bob Penniston's arms with his head resting on hers; they were sitting in the chaise longue from my dressing room. Ibrahim stood, eyes closed but erectly leaning against the dressing-room door, with Fatuoma held protectively against him, her eyes also closed. One can never get over the Arab's ability to sleep in any position whatever. . . .

In the far corner were Mr. Baker and Sir Percival, still in evening clothes and snoozing uncomfortably, with Gerson sitting drowsily on the floor. I was aware first of a twinge in my shoulders and wrist and a stiffness in my legs, but otherwise I felt disgustingly bright-eyed and beamish. Why not? I'd evidently had hours of good, fat sleep while everyone else was pacing the floor and wringing his hands.

I turned my head half an inch and found John uncomfortably cramped on the floor, his head pillowed against my hand, sleeping with the deep breaths of exhaustion. My instant reaction was indignation. How dared anyone let the poor boy sit on the floor?

Fingers gently raised my other hand. I looked up at a white-robed figure checking pulse rate against an efficient wristwatch and smiling at me calmly. "Doctor Livingstone, I presume?"

"Sorry; it's still Qeman, not darkest Africa, Mrs. Kennett."

"How'd I get here? I thought I was downstairs."

Dr. Amahl's dark eyes twinkled faintly as he laid my hand back on the coverlet. "Mr. Kennett carried you. Since there were no broken bones, we thought it wise to permit it." He shrugged. "It would have required a straitjacket to prevent, I assure you."

As I looked at my husband's tawny head resting against my hand, I felt him moving, disturbed by our voices. The room was coming to life. John opened his eyes blearily and came wide-awake when our eyes met. "Fran—oh, darling, you're alive!" He scrambled untidily to his knees and caught me in a hug, muttering between kisses, "You damn *fool*, if you ever do this again I'll throttle you, are you *sure* you're all right?"

"Yes, this is me—unless you squeeze me to a pulp." John loosened his hold slightly, and I looked up at his anxious face. Even with deep circles under his eyes, rumpled hair, beard stubble, he was handsome, but he could have had three eyes and been tinted a pale pea-green for all of me. I would still have loved him. It wasn't the moment to say so, with the room stirring and thrusting Dr. Amahl aside.

Nita made it first, ducking under his arm to see for herself I was okay. She exhaled a long, soft breath of relief and reacted typically. "Well! How dare you lie there looking fit as a fiddle, after the night you've put us through!"

"What night?" I returned callously. "You looked perfectly comfortable—trust you to find a soft berth for yourself."

"Of course. I never went to such a *dull* wake— no food, no dancing girls, nothing but moans and groans. But since you aren't dead, I suppose it doesn't matter."

"We can do it better when it's the real thing."

John was in no mood for levity. "Dammit, *quit* talking about death and wakes. Oh, Fran, *baby* . . ." He nearly suffocated me again.

"Please, darling," I gasped, "people are looking."

"Let them, and they should be ashamed of themselves. I paid two bucks for a piece of paper that says I can kiss you whenever and wherever I like."

"Madison Mines has a piece of paper you need more than kisses," Mr. Baker stated, "called a paycheck. Move aside, boy." He smiled down at me. "Thank God you're all right, Fran—*but where in hell IS the contract?*"

"Under the edge of the rug in John's study." I could sense hasty departure, jostling at the door, while the men streamed down the stairs. Then Fatuoma took over. "Is enough; you *go*. Madam eat, then dress, *then* talk." She would not allow even John to remain. When he was inclined to argue, she practically stamped her foot and stated, "Is all time for kissing; *now* madam must make ready."

"Whatever she means, I think she's got a point there," Nita observed irrepressibly. "Come along, John-boy. You could use a shave and shower yourself, to be fresh for all this kissing."

"Why can't I stay?" John complained. "Dammit, I'm afraid to take my eye off her. Heaven knows what she'll do next." Now that he knew I was safe, he was irritable with relief.

Ibrahim billowed forward. "You will be more comfortable in fresh clothing, Mr. Kennett." He swept John firmly toward his rooms. "And madam will do nothing to disturb you—there is nothing more for her to do."

The hell there isn't! I remembered, while Nita was staring after Ibrahim's masterly removal of John. "Do you suppose he handles his wife that easily?"

Fatuoma had come back from the bathroom, and for once she understood. "Ibrahim not married," she said, surprised. "Cousin of Sheikh."

"So what? The Sheikh is very much married."

"Is different. Sheikh find wife, Ibrahim not like; Ibrahim find wife, Sheikh not like." Fatuoma shrugged philosophically. "Ibrahim wait." She stripped back the covers, clucking sympathetically over my bruises.

"Poor Ibrahim!" Nita said.

"If you're so concerned for his welfare, perhaps His Highness would approve of you." I was discovering it was only my mind that felt okay—the rest of me was one big ache if I tried to use me. "How many camels d'you think would buy him? Ohhhhh!"

"Thanks, but I have other plans," Nita said thoughtfully. "See you later, sweetie."

I lay in the bathtub while Fatuoma fussed about in the bedroom, and I wondered vaguely what had happened to Ian. Had they caught him, or had he made good his escape? Where could he go? It seemed unlikely Abou ibn-Ferid would give him sanctuary without the contract terms. I *must* soak out enough stiffness to print Elvig's films. I knew now what they must reveal—Ian, conferring with the desert sheikh—although why that should cause murder? We all knew he was constantly in the desert—but perhaps he wasn't meant to be visiting that particular camp?

Eventually, Fatuoma got me out of the water, patted me dry, and authoritatively commanded me to lie upon the bed. She gave me a light but thorough massage, covered me up, and said, "Food now; you stay." I didn't, of course. As soon as she'd gone, I made for the darkroom. It was torture to move, but not quite so bad, and at sight of the negatives hanging where I'd left them, I half-forgot the twinges. *Please, God, let me not have ruined the things.*

I had one print before Fatuoma returned, and Ross was one hell of a photographer—only a complete fool could have failed with these—I'd been good enough. Every shot stood out clearly and unmistakably; more than that, the angles and lighting showed an imaginative artistry equal to Eisenstaedt. In contrast to Ross Elvig's crude outer personality, the revelation of his secret delicacy was both disarming and exciting beyond words. I remembered now that I'd had glimpses of it. I'd begun to find him less objectionable, had never liked him so well, as on the night he was killed.

By his choice of subjects, he was revealed—a shy man whose insight had been so compassionate that his only defense was a cocky brashness. I went out of the darkroom to gulp hot coffee, eat a slice of toast, and quiet Fatuoma. "*Why* you not rest? Eat; eat!"

"This is more important; they'll need it downstairs." I took a cup of coffee into the darkroom while I made the rest of the prints, and in the final group I had the reason for murder.

It was a series of portraits. Heaven knows how Ross had got them in the middle of the desert, with no lighting but sun or oil lamps, but each was superb . . . and among them was a clear picture of Ian Haysrath, bearded, wearing a *jibba*, seated cross-legged with Abou ibn-Ferid. They were laughing and clasping hands across a chessboard, and at a glance it was titled "The Good Deal."

The portrait was intended to be of the sheikh—Ian was merely part of the props and slightly turned from the camera—but there was no mistaking him . . . particulary when I remembered that afternoon and his teatime comment. He'd shaved the beard and left the mustache for Sheila's reaction, and I had said, "Weren't you devilish enough? You're gilding the lily."

But Ian had never expected to see the American photographer again—and Ross had not realized that Abou ibn-Ferid's companion wasn't part of the Bedouin camp. It was Ian Haysrath, in Western dinner clothes and without the beard, that Ross had vaguely recognized at the next table. Because he was a photographer, his eye had not been deceived by different surroundings; he'd known the bone structure. Before the end of the evening Ross had placed it—and whatever else he'd gleaned in the desert, he'd taken no chance.

Throughout Fatuoma's dressing me, carefully sliding blouse sleeves over my bruised arms and gently fastening hose to garter belt, that evening was coming back to me. Ross hadn't had the films in his traveler's dinner suit, of course—but when we left table, in the general hegira to the gents' and ladies' before settling in Hassim's rented chairs for Montalva's singing. Ross had gone to his own room and retrieved his undeveloped rolls. Plucky little guy, knowing the danger, yet determined to help if he could. . . .

In a way, Ross Elvig had given his life for his country, though he might not get a medal. Studying the prints, I was determined he'd get *some* sort of posthumous recognition for his gift. *Life* magazine would help; there could be a special showing of Elvig photographs . . . *something*. I'd insist on it, tell the State Department to speak to Henry Luce . . . once the story behind the story was known, everyone would agree.

"Waiting," Fatuoma warned, anxiously. "Please, you come?"

"Yes." She'd be blamed for stupidity and inefficiency if I delayed too long when she'd made every effort to get me ready for the questions. "Don't worry; I'll explain it's not your fault, Fatuoma." I stood up, clutching the prints and groaning involuntarily. Every step was an effort. I made it to the hall door, but the sight of the stairs . . .

"Can you make it if I brace you on the other side?" Nita asked.

"God knows, but I have to get down somehow."

"Miss Janus, if you please . . ." Ibrahim gently pushed her away. "With your permission, madam." Well, I am a *large*, healthy American woman, but Ibrahim picked me up like an infant and merely walked down the stairs with no visible sign of strain. Halfway down I had an idea.

"Hadn't you better marry Fatuoma? I could ask Mr. Baker to speak to His Highness."

For the first time, Ibrahim grinned broadly. "Thank you, madam; the matter is already under consideration."

"What's holding it up? If she hasn't enough goats or camels, we'll buy them."

"That will not be necessary, madam." I could feel his arms shaking slightly. "But she will appreciate the offer."

"I don't want to mix into your marital affairs, but hadn't you better tell her? She doesn't seem to know she's under consideration."

"A point well taken, madam, but she is still young, after all. One prefers these things to develop gradually."

"Oh, piffle. If you're not careful, someone else will snap her up—and stop being so *repressive*," I said crossly.

Ibrahim stood still in the lower hall, looking

down at me. "Yes; John said we should tell you everything," he remarked, "but His Highness is of the old school and has no understanding of the American woman—*Frances*." He quivered with silent laughter at my expression. Before I could find my voice, I was carefully deposited on the couch, with Fatuoma fluttering around to spread a light shawl over my feet and arrange a pillow under my head. Ibrahim bowed politely and retreated before the concerted rush of people.

"Sorry to disturb you, but we must have answers, Mrs. Kennett. Why did you suspect Mr. Haysrath, why did you come home alone last night, how did you know where the contract was?"

"Please," I said, "don't everybody speak at once. Sit down, and I'll tell you." Out of the corner of my eye I could see Nita gravitating toward Bob Penniston like a magnet. Hmmm, so *he* was her plans?

John bent over me. "Are you really up to it, darling?"

"Of course—but first I have a question," I said steadily, meeting Sir Percival's eyes. He was gray with fatigue, devastated, but still able to square his shoulders in the sudden silence.

"Ian Haysrath is . . . dead, Mrs. Kennett," he told me formally.

"I can't be sorry, Sir Percival," I said after a moment. "I'm sure suicide was preferable to . . . hanging, or a gas chamber, or whatever you do to murderers in England." There was a collective indrawn breath, and Old Perce looked grayer than ever. "Didn't you know? Ian killed Ross Elvig. . . ." I held out the prints, and they were swiftly passed from hand to hand.

Gerson said, "Why didn't you tell me, where did you get these?"

"Because I didn't know. I only found them yesterday—they were in my evening bag. Ross must have put them there, but Fatuoma took the bag away for fear I'd be distressed to see it." I smiled mirthlessly. "She got hit on the head for her pains, poor child. I could put two and two together, know what the thief wanted—but I knew only that I didn't have Ross's films. And Fatuoma never knew there was anything but the usual makeup in my purse, because she was too honorable to open it."

"Why did you suspect Haysrath? Begin at the beginning, Fran?" Mr. Baker smiled at me

"I didn't suspect Ian—I thought it was—" I stopped short. "Well, I'll apologize to him personally, but I thought it was Gregor, even though John said the Russians didn't fit."

They let it pass tactfully. "How did you know where the contract was?" Gerson asked.

"I was looking for something to make a costume for the fancy dress party next week."

John sighed deeply. "After we'd been searched," he told Baker, "I put it in the bottom drawer of a storage bureau. I should have known better, but my God, could I expect her to be rummaging around in woolen underwear?"

"No; of course not. Very undependable, women," Sir Percival agreed absently. "Always ferreting about, turning out drawers and closets when least expected . . . but why did you come back without telling anyone, Frances?"

"Because I never had a chance to tell John I'd found it. And Nita—oh, she didn't know how it'd sound, but at dinner, she said a woman hides things in her bureau drawer, and I knew by Gregor's eyes he'd *understood.* I dropped my napkin, but he knew *I* knew the contract *was* in a drawer."

"I never *dreamed,*" Nita said, horrified. "Oh, I could tell you wanted the conversation *away* from the burglar, but I had no idea *why* . . . and I never knew anyone was killed."

"I didn't tell you, because I thought the less you knew, the more you'd innocently confuse the issue . . . and last night, I couldn't even tell you to tell Bob to tell John I needed to speak to him. I couldn't get a minute alone with *anyone.*" My eyes blurred with tears. "I thought we'd be able to leave after the entertainment, but Sir Percival wanted to play bridge . . . and just when he was nearly finished, Mr. Baker was making up another table. I thought we were going to be there *all night,*" I wailed, "and after Bob made Sheila drunk, so she exploded when I didn't want her to . . . I went back to the phone booth, and Gregor wasn't there . . . and I called Ibrahim, but there wasn't any answer.

"So, when Mrs. Tomyienkov and madame

Beyda came upstairs to the loo, I went down the back stairs and came home," I finished confusedly. "I thought if the contract was gone, I could at least break the news before expected . . . but I should have realized, when I saw Ian with Abou ibn-Ferid."

"*What?* When was this?"

"At the airport, the day Nita arrived. I didn't know it was Ian until I saw him walking that evening. And I didn't know the sheikh at all, but it was the same man in the back room at Azriel's."

"Good Lord!" Mr. Baker closed his eyes. "My God, John, what were you thinking of!"

"I never knew she went there," John protested, harrassed. "Dammit, you wouldn't let me tell her anything, and Ibrahim was supposed to look after her."

"He tried," I put in, before Ibrahim could defend himself, "but I got away from him . . . and he didn't know I'd always meant to visit that shop because I'd seen Ross Elvig coming out of the place." Ibrahim straightened up to full height, staring at me. "I'm sorry, Ibrahim, I know you kept tabs on everything, and you kept me away from Azriel that first day, but I thought it was only that you knew I'd spend too much time in the *souk*, when I was supposed to be throwing my weight around in the market."

"I apologize, Mr. Kennett," Ibrahim said resignedly, "but I did not see Mr. Elvig until he approached the car. Even when he returned to Qeman, it was merely reported that he'd been seen

in the *souk*. We never connected him with Azriel—
his caravan arrangements were completely legiti-
mate. If madam had said—"

"Why should I? For all *I* knew, until you got me
out of that demonstration, you were simply a native butler, selling the jobs and getting a kickback
from the tradesmen."

There was a long, appalled silence, while the
company digested my view of His Highness's
Harvard-educated cousin. "Well, if you never told
her anything, I should say '*touché*—and what else
could you expect her to think?" Nita observed dis-
passionately.

"Well, I suppose it's to your credit to have
fooled her," Mr. Baker said heavily, "but I'd like a
straight story, instead of skipping about. You seem
to know a number of things we don't, Frances.
Please go back to the beginning, wherever the hell
it is," he finished morosely.

"Well, I suppose it starts when John didn't
really want me, but I came anyway."

Instant sensation! "What are you talking about?
Dammit, d'you think I liked being here alone?"
John's voice rolled over the room. "I was thinking
of your safety; I didn't want you in the middle of
whatever was going on—and how right I was!" he
added bitterly. "You no sooner get off the plane
than you're involved with this photographer who's
assigned to cover the very person His Highness
most distrusts. Inside of two weeks, you've got
Haysrath hanging around here every day for tea—
the very man we're keeping a check on! It's taking

all my time to convince his wife you're not under-cutting her, and on top of that, you turn up yell-ing in a garden with a corpse at your feet!"

Sir Percival cleared his throat slightly. "A very expectable reaction, John. Shockin' sight, what? Covered with blood and all that, what?" He con-sulted Baker with a glance and finished firmly, "Finds a dead body, opens her mouth and screams—perfectly normal female reaction. Sur-prised she didn't faint; they usually do."

"Dammit!" John was shouting. "My wife isn't 'normal'—she's *intelligent*, not that you could prove it by the last few weeks."

He turned toward me, but before he could say anything, I cut in, "Please darling—couldn't I just tell what happened?" I asked wistfully.

"Yes! For God's sake, John, sit *down*." Baker's voice was firm. "You can straighten out your pri-vate affairs later, but I've got to have a story for His Highness in an hour. Go on, Fran."

Slowly, John backed away and sat down, but by the look in his eye, I wasn't in any hurry to finish up and be left alone with him. Once more, and I hoped for the last time, I went through the whole thing—from talking with Ross on the plane, to his murder, to Fatuoma's bash on the head, to Azriel's anxiety to be rid of us.

"*Why*, Mrs. Kennett?"

"Because he recognized a voice that came in to the backroom party while Nita was buying a bracelet, and he thought I'd recognize it too. After that, he stopped bargaining—he couldn't wait to get us out of the place. He practically gave Nita the most beautiful rug, in order to get us away from the rug curtains at the rear."

"But who was it, Mrs. Kennett?"

"That's the hell of it," I said miserably. "I still don't know, except that I heard it again at the party—and I thought it must be Gregor, but later I knew it wasn't."

"In heaven's name, *how!*" Baker was practically shouting at me.

"Because when I went to call Ibrahim, Gregor was in the phone booth talking to his girlfriend in Arabic . . . and it wasn't the same intonation."

There was a long pause. I could see Fouad bringing in fresh coffee and a basket of that delicious Levantine bread that is like chapaties, while Baker closed his eyes with a groan, running his hands distractedly through the remains of his hair. "My God, John, I don't wonder you didn't want her here," he said hoarsely. "How in hell did she get onto Fawzia and Gregor? What am I to say to His Highness?"

"Why should he care who Gregor's courting?" I asked shakily. "I never heard her name, but if you know it, you can bet Berthe Drouet does too. What's so secret?"

"Only that Fawzia is my younger sister," Ibrahim said calmly, "and it will be more comfortable if her choice of husband is approved by His Highness. We have been waiting for a . . . suitable moment to place the matter before him."

I closed my eyes and shivered mentally. Thank

heavens I hadn't said I'd thought Gregor was talking to his mistress! "Have some coffee, Fran?"
Nita extended the cup. There was a faint buzz of
conversation behind her. While I was trying to
think what to say, I distinctly heard The Voice.

"There it is!" I rolled over on the couch and
stared about wildly. "Who was speaking Arabic,
just now this minute . . . *who?*"

"What are you talking about, Fran?"

"The Voice," I cried wildly. "The voice I heard
at Azriel's, the voice he thought I'd recognize."
Out of the corner of my eye, I caught unobtrusive
movement. "Fouad . . . that's who it was. He
was serving drinks last night; it was his voice I
heard."

There was a slight scuffle, and Ibrahim had col-
lared Fouad with one hand and dragged him back
into the room as though holding a puppy by the
scruff of the neck. Encircled by the men striding
forward, Fouad went to pieces at once, screaming
in a high falsetto like a cornered rabbit, although
no one laid a finger on him, aside from Ibrahim. It
was all Arabic, and apparently whenever he didn't
answer satisfactorily, Ibrahim simply gave him a
slight shake, which produced instant results.

I went to pieces too, until Nita produced a
handkerchief for mopping my eyes. "Pull around,
kiddie—it's nearly over," she said calmly. "Wow,
that Ibrahim! You wouldn't think a Harvard man
could be so untamed, after four years of The
Yard."

Eventually, Fouad was turned over to a local

policeman, and everybody came back to me, but there was a subtle difference.

"Fran, I haven't time now to tell you, but you've settled something." Mr. Baker shook his head and patted my hand warmly. "When I tell His Highness . . ." He shook his head again, grinning. "He'll never underestimate American women again, I can tell you!" He bent over and kissed me heartily. "I'm off to the palace—John, stay by the phone, in case I need you."

He shook hands with Sir Percival, who was looking much more perky, and vanished into the hall, with Gerson behind him. Old Perce came over to me; he was still a bit gray but able to square his shoulders with relief. "I must go, too . . . but Frances, I thank you from the bottom of my heart. You're a gallant spirit, even if you can't play bridge." He smiled at me.

After he left, I looked at Nita. "What 'n hell was this in aid of?" I asked dazedly. "Wha' happened? One moment they're all over me for Miss Dumkopf of the year . . . and the next, they're giving me verbal roses."

"Don't ask me." Nita shrugged. "I think it was when you fingered Fouad, but I couldn't understand what they were saying either. Don't worry about it, sweetie. No doubt the explanation will be forthcoming in due course." She lit two cigarettes, stuck one neatly in my hand, and squinted reflectively. "I wonder if they'll give Fouad a bath in jail?"

I smoked silently for a moment. "I feel I've

been the most complete fool . . . Ian's dead, and
Fouad in jail," I said desperately, "and all for
nothing, really. I dragged you into a nasty scene,
and what's to become of Sheila and the two children? Oh, Nita, why was I so stupid?"

"Don't blame yourself," Nita said quietly. "The
end was inevitable; we merely . . . hastened it.
Bob says they always suspected Ian. He and
Sheila have been working this game for years, but
it was always small potatoes until now. This time
the stake was considerable, worth a murder."

"How come you know all this and I don't?" I
asked suspiciously. "Why is Bob confiding in
you?"

"Because I have a high IQ and a beautiful soul,
natch," she said, getting up from the edge of my
couch. "We need a clean ashtray."

"Why? We haven't half-used the one we
have."

"No more we have," she said brightly, sitting
down again and eyeing me with a grin.

"All right, I won't addle the eggs," I said resignedly, "but I'm beginning to feel like that For-
syte character who was forever saying nobody
told him anything."

"What would you like to be told?" John inquired deeply, leaning over the end of the couch.

"Everything," I said promptly, "and will you
please come around front where I can see you?
I've enough aches and pains without a crick in the
neck."

He circled about and knelt down beside me, putting his arms around me. "That better?"

"Infinitely. You may kiss me," I decided graciously. After a moment, "Not so *hard;* I'm only a fragile female."

John laughed, loosening his hold slightly. "Oh, honey—I'll never be able to tell you how wonderful you were. It was all much more than even we suspected, and why you weren't killed . . ." He shook his head sickly.

"Well, I wasn't—but unless somebody explains something, I'll die of suspense. Where was Ibrahim, and why did you come to the rescue? I suppose it was Fouad who knocked Fatuoma on the head?"

"Yes." John's lips tightened grimly. "Fouad was actually more important than Ian . . . and we never had a smell of him until you identified his voice. Oh, we knew he was a son of Abou ibn-Ferid, but there's a dozen number one sons ahead of him. He never even lived in the desert; his mother was a Qemani girl Abou married on one of his trips to town—and divorced her Moslem style before he went back to the desert. Fouad had a decent reputation; nobody ever connected him with the rear room at Azriel's shop or knew he had any contact with his father."

"You mean that horrid little spiv is Fatuoma's *cousin?*" Nita asked incredulously.

"Yes, but she's not concerned in any of this . . . and if it comes to that, half of Qeman is related to everybody else," John went on, "including the

Sheikh and Abou—they're first cousins. Maybe that's what gave Fouad delusions of grandeur. Apparently he figured to dethrone Sulieman in favor of Abou, thus putting himself into the number-one-son spot, and the oil contract was a perfect tool—as well as Ian Haysrath.

"Ian's had a shaky reputation for years. Nothing was ever proved, but there's no doubt he's been mixed up in a succession of shady deals in every post he's held. Sheila helped him—I don't know how much she knew, but she did whatever he told her. Mostly, her job was to get next to whatever man might be useful for whatever Ian had in mind." John squinted into space judicially. "She didn't do it very well, but she was only a country girl, after all. I expect she was competent enough until she hit the big league."

I looked expressionlessly at Nita's twitching eyebrows. "I see. Go on, darling."

"Well, Fouad used Ian to make contact with his father. Ian could go out to the desert. He wasn't supposed to be with Abou when Elvig was filming—you were right about that, Fran—but he'd been there legitimately many other times. He took messages back and forth and made a deal on his own with Abou for a handsome sum if he could deliver the oil contract terms before signing. Fouad didn't mind—he was playing for higher stakes.

"If *he* could put his father in the palace, he'd outrank the older sons, d'you see? Fouad stood to wind up in the peacock seat. Abou's nearly eighty;

he's always been jealous of Sulieman, and he'd be receptive to any suggestion of getting himself on the throne, even for only a few years. And he's filthy rich, well able to pay for *anything* that might help. Ian was the perfect go-between, and Fouad didn't care how much money he made so long as the coup materialized."

John grinned at me. "You said *I* didn't want you—which was a damned lie," he remarked, "but the person who really didn't want you was Fouad. You loused him up, but good!"

"How? I hardly ever saw him," I protested, "aside from that first day I went marketing to throw my weight around to create 'face' for the household."

"But you were *here*, all the time," Bob said quietly, sitting down beside Nita, "and you knew that Ross Elvig who was assigned to photograph Fouad's father's desert camp. You went places, met people, entertained guests." He smiled. "Don't you understand? When John was here alone, the household had nothing to do but make him comfortable. When you arrived, it meant everyone had to be on his toes all the time, including Fouad."

"Naturally." Nita nodded her head. "Fran's a great one for noticing dust."

"She's much better at noticing more important things," John said loyally. "If she hadn't remembered Fouad's voice, we'd still be nowhere, except with another corpse on our hands."

"What do you mean?" I asked, after a moment.

"You'll have to know," he said. "Bob missed you at the party, and Nita found your wrap gone. That's why we rushed back. We heard you screaming, and Bob and I came through the front, Nita went around through the garden, and Ian came tearing out of the study window. She threw the big clay water bottle under his feet."

"He came down with a frightful thud," Nita said calmly, "so then I whanged him on the head with a flower pot. I'm afraid they're both broken to bits, Fran, but I had to leave him until I could open the study door for the boys. And of course you were lying on the floor looking like Ophelia, so we wasted a bit of time making sure you weren't dead. By the time Bob went out to look at Ian," she said, her voice shaking slightly, "*he* turned out to be dead. Someone had stuck a knife in him."

"Fouad?" I whispered, appalled.

"He hasn't admitted it yet, but there's no doubt. He set the scene for Ian when he was dismissed after dinner. He came back here secretly—Ibrahim never saw him—and doctored the servants' coffee-pot. Fatuoma got less than Zoe and Ibrahim; she only had one cup, so she heard the shot. She knew something was going on, but she couldn't wake Ibrahim until it was all over." John patted my shoulder gently. "Don't think about it now, darling."

"That's why the front light was turned out and the study windows were unfastened," I said absently, "and how can I *not* think about it? I feel like a . . . Jonah. Or do I mean Judas? Two men dead because of me, a nasty scandal for Sir Percival to cope with, and what's to become of Sheila and the kids? Oh, I *wish* I'd never come, or sent for Nita," I wailed. "I should have left well enough alone. You'd have managed perfectly without me, if you always knew it was Ian."

"Stop Gummidging, darling," Nita said. "Ian got what was coming to him, and he'd have killed Elvig somehow, some way, even if you'd never been here. If anything, you were Nemesis, the X-factor of bad luck. Without you, Elvig's films would have been found and destroyed. Fouad would still be conniving. If he couldn't use the contract as a focal point, he'd have found something else to create a real rumpus . . . and until you fingered him, nobody ever knew he was masterminding, not even Ibrahim. And finally"—she grinned wickedly—"Bob and I are damned glad you sent for me. So there!"

I absorbed her comfortable position against Bob's shoulder, the interlocked hands, the blissful expression on his unremarkable face. "When's the wedding?"

"Next week," she said blandly. "Care to come?"

John suddenly came to life. "Dammit, Penniston, the least you could have done was ask me for her hand! I'm responsible for this flighty minded wench as long as she's in my household—and that's another thing"—he turned on me—"why did you 'send' for Nita?"

"I thought she'd enjoy a change from Greek islands," I said. "Well, now it's all explained, could we forget it for a while? My head's aching like fury."

"Mmmm." John looked at Bob. "Disappear," he said tersely.

"I'm really all right, if you'd just ask Fatuoma for some aspirin," I said hastily. "They don't need to go."

"Oh, yes they do," John said firmly. "He's got his girl—I'd like a word with mine."

Bob was already on his feet, drawing Nita toward the garden. When they were gone, John said, "All right, out with it: why did you 'send' for Nita? Could it be that you were *worried* about Sheila Haysrath?"

I could feel myself flushing wildly, until John laughed. He pulled my chin toward him and kissed me soundly. "Sometimes you're a silly goose," he murmured affectionately. "Don't you *know* you're the only woman in the world I want forever?"

"I don't know that I do," I admitted honestly. "I never knew what there was about me to get you in the first place . . . and I am *not* a jealous bitch, John. I'd be heartbroken to lose you, but if you found someone you liked better than me, I'd let you go. I wouldn't even be surprised."

"You wouldn't lift a finger to keep me?" he protested, deeply wounded. "Like sending for Nita, or telling the consul's daughter to go back to college and getting me out of that tangle with the widow in Mozambique?" He grinned at my stunned expression. "Think I didn't know? One of the reasons I love you so dearly-dearly: you've got such a level head. I'm one man who'll never be able to say, 'My wife doesn't understand me'—which is why I don't understand your sending for Nita."

"It was a momentary . . . aberration."

"Not good enough. Nothing less than full disclosure, sweetheart."

"Oh, well, if you *will* have it," I said despairingly, "I saw you kissing her in the Argentine garden—madame Drouet saw you too—and," I gulped, "it made me mad. I didn't know how you felt about her, but I was certain she didn't give a hoot for anyone but Ian. I sent for Nita to work on him until something exploded . . . but it was useless, because he didn't really want a rich wife. He wanted Sheila, because he could bang her around and tell her what to do."

"If you could figure that out, why on earth did you worry?" John asked. "It was perfectly true, you know. I was only playing along with her to find out whatever I could, and she was doing the same thing with me. Baker told me Drouet had tipped him this was the way Haysrath worked. And we weren't getting anywhere, either, which was why Bob decided to get her drunk."

I hung my head silently, until John commanded, "Let's have the rest of it."

"I wasn't sure how *you* felt," I whispered. "You didn't really want me to come—you said I was too forthright and uncompromising, and I thought perhaps you might be wanting someone . . . oh, softer, less efficient, or something."

John looked at me incredulously. "Good God," he said finally, "don't you know you're the reason I've gone ahead so fast? Don't you know you're the standard they use for all other overseas wives?" I shook my head dumbly. "Well, take my word for it." He smiled. "It needs a special kind of wife to cope uncomplainingly with jungles and pythons, to pack and unpack, make a home in a treetop if needed, and most of all, keep her husband contented." John looked me straight in the eye. "I never saw another girl I wanted. I can appreciate a pretty, intelligent woman—I'd have to be dead if I didn't—but I've never met one who could tempt me above you. I'm depressingly faithful, darling."

"Oh, dear, so am I . . . and I don't even think other men are worth appreciating." I sighed, sadly.

John leaned over and kissed me, then laid his face next to mine, and we were silent for a while. Dimly I could hear soft voices cooing in the garden. The air was still and dry. Somewhere a native was singing one of those mournful wails that pass for love music in Arabia. I turned and kissed John lingeringly. "Now that we really understand each other, and since I'm such a perfect wife, do I *still* have to wait two years to start a baby?"

A love forged by destiny—
A passion born of flame

FLAMES OF DESIRE

by Vanessa Royall

Selena MacPherson, a proud princess of ancient
Scotland, had never met a man who did not desire
her. From the moment she met Royce Campbell at
an Edinburgh ball, Selena knew the burning
ecstasy that was to seal her fate through all eternity.
She sought him on the high seas, in India, and
finally in a young America raging in the
birth-throes of freedom, where destiny was bound
to fulfill its promise. . . .

A DELL BOOK $1.95

The irresistible love story with a happy ending.

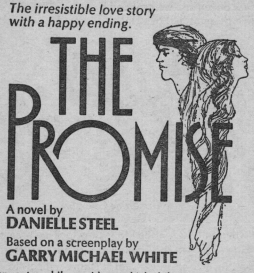

THE PROMISE

A novel by
DANIELLE STEEL

Based on a screenplay by
GARRY MICHAEL WHITE

After an automobile accident which left Nancy McAllister's beautiful face a tragic ruin, she accepted the money for plastic surgery from her lover's mother on one condition: that she never contact Michael again. She didn't know Michael would be told that she was dead.

Four years later, Michael met a lovely woman whose face he didn't recognize, and wondered why she hated him with such intensity . . .

A Dell Book $1.95

She was driven into womanhood by the
terrible passions that ruled men's hearts.

the Slow Awakening

by **Catherine Cookson**
writing as **Catherine Marchant**

The author of <u>Miss Martha Mary Crawford</u> has created
another passionate and endearing heroine in Kirsten
McGregor, an orphan who had to learn early how to survive
brutal hardships. As a young woman, she was sold into
servitude to a cruel and elderly tinker. The whim of harsh
destiny forced Kirsten to carry the child of her vicious
master and face the threat of death. Worse still was the
secret which prevented her from achieving happiness with
the one man who could awaken her lonely heart! "A
wonderfully engrossing tale. Catherine Cookson-Marchant
casts her usual spell with passions and people, and as always,
her novel ends much too soon."—Publishers Weekly

A Dell Book $1.95

Dell Bestsellers

"A gripping heartwarming novel!" –Publishers Weekly

THE HOUSE OF CHRISTINA

by BEN HAAS

As the threat of Nazi tyranny spread across Vienna in 1938, only the boldest of hearts, the greatest of loves would survive. Young, beautiful, frivolous Christa Helmer, mistress of the House of Christina, and Lan Condon, an American journalist who found respite from personal tragedy in Austria, are determined to reunite despite the Nazi menace. Theirs is a love you will always remember, from a time the world will never forget.

"Beautiful! Marvelously depicted characters. It deserves to be an enormous bestseller!"—Taylor Caldwell

A Dell Book $2.25